Silent Night Dynamite

A Spicetown Mystery

Sheri Richey

Sheri Richey

For further information, contact the publisher: Cagelink

ISBN: 978-0-578-25889-8

Front Cover art by Mariah Sinclair of The Cover Vault

Spicetown Mysteries

Welcome to Spicetown

A Bell in the Garden

Spilling the Spice

Blue Collar Bluff

A Tough Nut to Crack

Chicory is Trickery

The No Dill Zone

Cons & Quinces

Romance by Sheri Richey:

The Eden Hall Series:
Finding Eden
Saving Eden
Healing Eden
Protecting Eden
Completing Eden

∞

Willow Wood
Knight Events

Sheri Richey

Silent Night ♫

Silent night, holy night!
All is calm, all is bright.
Round yon Virgin, Mother and Child.
Holy infant so tender and mild,
Sleep in heavenly peace,
Sleep in heavenly peace

Silent night, holy night!
Shepherds quake at the sight.
Glories stream from heaven afar
Heavenly hosts sing Alleluia,
Christ the Savior is born!
Christ the Savior is born

Silent night, holy night!
Son of God love's pure light.
Radiant beams from Thy holy face
With dawn of redeeming grace,
Jesus Lord, at Thy birth
Jesus Lord, at Thy birth

Josephus Franciscus Mohr

Sheri Richey

Chapter 1

"Good morning, ladies!" Harvey "Saucy" Salzman, hopped across the threshold of Amanda Morgan's office and held his arms out to each side. His grin lit up the room when Mayor Cora Mae Bingham gasped. His startling entrance was aimed with that exact reaction in mind.

"Goodness, Saucy! You appeared out of thin air. What mischief are you up to this morning?"

Amanda Morgan giggled when Saucy wiggled his eyebrows.

"Just paid my water bill," Saucy said, pointing toward the lobby of City Hall. "I saw you were both in here whispering about city secrets and I decided to pop in." Saucy nodded and pulled his scarf tighter around his neck. "Got anything juicy today?"

"Not juicy," Amanda said with a shrug, "but delicious! I was just telling the mayor about my cake tasting experiment. My girlfriend and I went over to Paxton and sampled some different cakes and icing last weekend. I'm looking for something special for my wedding cake."

"That sounds yummy!" Saucy let his gloved hands slap against the sides of his coat. "My favorite is raspberry with cream cheese icing. My sister, June, used to make me one every year for my birthday. It's too much work for her nowadays though. You can't get something that fancy from a box. She made it from the ground up and it was always delicious! She just tells me now that I don't need to eat sweets and to stop thinking about it. I bring it up every year. It's a good birthday memory."

"That does sound good." Amanda picked up a list she had in her day planner. "I think we may have sampled one like that."

"The cream cheese icing is really good on spice cake, too." Cora winked at Saucy. "Spice cake is my favorite."

"I do see a raspberry," Amanda said tapping the list. "It didn't have cream cheese icing though. I might have to suggest that."

"You know, Amanda," Cora said pointing her finger at her. "You don't need to go to Paxton for a wedding cake."

Saucy nodded. "Vicki can make anything you like. Her cakes are beautiful."

"Once you decide on the flavor you want, you should drop in the Fennel Street Bakery and see what she can offer. I bet she beats the prices in Paxton and it sure would be easier to have your cake here in town close to the reception when you are trying to get everything ready." Cora took a few steps back to turn Amanda's visitor chair around to sit in. She had been struggling more and more lately with the pain in her knees and really couldn't stand in one place for long periods. The cold and wet winter weather was not offering any comfort.

"Really?" Amanda's forehead furrowed. "Are you

sure? I didn't think she did cakes at all. Just donuts and bread. I've never seen any cakes in there."

"She has a book!" Saucy held up a finger. "Ask her to show it to you. It's full of pictures of cakes she's made for people over the years. When my stepdaughter opened her business, I bought her grand opening day cake from Vicki, and I looked through the book. There were lots of wedding cakes in there. Tall ones, short ones, cakes that look like toys and animals, all different kinds."

"Wow! Well, I will definitely check with her then." Amanda scribbled a note in her planner. There was so much still to do.

"You just let us know." Cora patted Saucy's arm. "We are both here to help."

"Sure thing!" Saucy rocked up on his toes and smiled.

"Saucy, speaking of helping out, how is the Christmas play coming? Did you decide to audition or are you just helping out this time?"

"Well," Saucy hung his head low and pulled the word out until it was three-syllables long. "My intention was to just offer support, but somehow or another I got roped into another role. It's a short one. Should be easy to memorize and I'm already working on it. This year I get to be a barber!"

"A barber! Do you know anything about being a barber?" Cora Mae smiled.

"No, but I think they're afraid to give me real scissors anyway." Saucy shrugged and shook his head. "I play a barber named Will and I work with my three brothers who are barbers, too. I'm not the owner. That's played by Walter Slope. He is my brother, Sam. Then there's Bert Miller and Otis

Scarsdale playing my other two brothers."

Cora Mae frowned. "I don't know Walter Slope. Is this a musical? It sounds like a barbershop quartet." Cora Mae shrugged and looked at Amanda. "How often do you have four barbers?"

"Now, you'll just have to come watch to find that out!" Saucy tossed his head back and laughed.

"Hmm," Cora Mae pinched her chin. She was pretty certain Saucy couldn't sing a lick.

"What's this Christmas play called?" Amanda turned toward her computer monitor with her fingers poised over the keyboard, ready to pull up the Spicetown Star newspaper. "I thought the paper said it was going to be *A Christmas Carol* this year."

"That's what Eleanor Cline wanted to do, but the version she had required a lot of male actors to fill those roles and we just didn't have many men show up for auditions. That's how I got roped into a role again."

"So, what did Eleanor choose instead?" Cora's eyebrows raised.

"A Comfort Falls Christmas."

"I've not heard of that one." Cora shook her head and looked at Amanda, who also shook her head. "What's it about?"

"I'm not spoiling the surprise." Saucy straightened his posture. "You will just have to wait until opening day."

"Or Amanda can look it up." Cora chuckled and pointed at Amanda's computer monitor.

"Resist!" Saucy held his hand up as if to stop traffic. "Let the show embrace the season in true Spicetown fashion."

Cora leaned back in her chair and laughed. "Oh,

Saucy. You were made for the theater!"

"I'm trying to get into character," Saucy said sheepishly. "Oh, look! There's Walter. You said you didn't know him." Saucy waved his hand at the lobby and then urged the man closer. "Hey, Walter. Let me introduce you to the mayor."

Walter Slope stood in the doorway of Amanda's office as Cora Mae stood up.

"Mayor Bingham, this is Walter Slope. He's fairly new in town, only been here about... what? Maybe two or three months." Saucy urged Walter to step closer, and he extended his hand to reach Cora's.

"This is Miss Amanda Morgan." Saucy waved Walter's attention toward Amanda and she nodded at Walter from behind her desk monitor.

"Nice to meet you," Amanda said.

Walter removed the toothpick from his mouth. "Lovely to meet you both! I was just coming in today specifically to stop in and meet you. Thank you for helping me do that, Harvey."

"Glad to help! I was just telling the ladies about this year's Christmas play. They'll ask you a million questions, so be careful. Don't give away the secrets because I want to make sure they show up to see the play." Saucy shook his index finger at Walter.

Walter pretended to lock his lips with an imaginary key. "Not a word."

"You mentioned music, Mayor." Saucy nodded in Cora's direction. "Eleanor did work out something with the middle school choir. The kids are going to sing Christmas carols at the opening and closing of the performance from inside the auditorium instead of the lobby this year, so there will be a lot of Christmas music. Don't you worry!"

"Wonderful, Saucy! I'm excited to see it. I know you'll both do a fabulous job."

"Thank you, Mayor. Well, I must be off. Merry Christmas, everyone." Saucy waved a gloved hand as he backed out of Amanda's office door and Cora looked quizzically at Walter.

"You said you needed to see me?"

"Yes, if you have a minute." Walter reached inside his coat as Cora Mae rose from her chair.

"Let's go in my office."

Walter smiled and nodded to Amanda as he passed by, following Cora to her desk. "I wanted to introduce myself. I've been in town for some time now and I've intended every day to stop in. It's just been so busy with moving, a new job, and accidentally signing up for a community play." Walter chuckled.

"It was an accident?"

"I saw the advertisement regarding auditions for *A Christmas Carol*. I have been in the play several times and already know the lines for two of the ghosts, so I went to the audition thinking it would be a good way to meet others in town. I didn't expect to end up in a new play that would require me to learn new lines." Walter shrugged his shoulders. "Harvey has been very helpful and one of my employees is also in the play. Do you know Otis Scarsdale?"

"I do. He works at the mines," Cora said. "Is that where you are working now?"

"Yes, oh, I guess I should have led with that." Walter smiled. "I was transferred here to the Paxton Mine. The previous manager was moved to another of the company's properties. They shift us around sometimes to meet particular needs."

"I know that they have changed numerous times,

but I've rarely met the managers. The mine is not within our city limits, so unless there is an inquiry or a problem, I haven't had reason to reach out to the mine management." Cora dropped her shoulders and took a deep breath. She could not imagine why Mr. Slope felt the need to introduce himself, but he was very pleasant, and he exuded a peacefulness that Cora found relaxing.

"I hope for this to be my last assignment. I am nearing my golden retirement days and wistfully planning for a future lifestyle that might just include Spicetown. I played here as a child and have fond memories of the town. My grandparents lived here, so I spent my summers staying with them, to free up my parents to tend their farm. When I got a little older, my folks put me to work, but those early days with my grandparents are my favorite time."

"I remember a Mr. Slope who worked at the dairy." Cora's eyes squinted. She could see him in her memories as he came up the sidewalk.

"Yes, that was my grandfather. He delivered milk. I always wanted to go with him, but he never would let me." Walter chuckled. "They had a small farm at the edge of town, just enough for them. I could help in the garden and collect their eggs. They were good people."

"Well, there are still good people in this town. I think you will find it just as pleasant as you did as a child. I wouldn't live anywhere else!" Cora tapped her fist on her desk softly.

"I am finding that to be true." Reaching inside his coat again, Walter pulled out a sheet of paper folded lengthwise. Opening it, he handed it across the desk to Cora. "This is just an amended blast notice. I've had to adjust the times a bit, nothing alarming, just a requirement that I notify the community. I have asked the newspaper to print a notice also but wanted to drop off a copy for you as a courtesy. I hope it doesn't inconvenience anyone."

"The mine is going to be blasting?" Cora slipped on her reading glasses and perused the notice. "I can tell you that the community does speak out from time to time. I hope it is not going to be too frequent. With the holidays just around the corner, citizens may be more inclined than usual to protest the disruptions."

"Perhaps the reason will be soothing." Walter raised his eyebrows. "The blasting is being done to close a number of underground tunnels that are in disrepair or infrequently used. Although it may cause some temporary disturbance now, it will eliminate the need for additional blasting in those areas, thus reducing the overall future impact."

Cora Mae glanced at Walter over the top of her glasses. He was a fancy speaker, but that type of schmoozing didn't go unchallenged by her. "So, you are reducing the size of the mine. Perhaps that will mean reducing the size of the staff as well? I assure you that this will also be met with resistance from the citizens. That mine is a source of income for many in our community."

"Oh, no. You misunderstand me, Mayor. I am trying to turn the mine around, make it more profitable, help it to grow. Reducing staff is not my plan at all. I am a fixer, and I was sent here to improve the working situation, cut costs, and make the mine a positive producer for the company. The only downside is the needed blasting and the unfortunate timing of that disruption during the holiday season. I'm hoping the community will be understanding."

Cora Mae removed her glasses and stood up from her desk chair. "I can't promise you anything, Mr. Slope, but I will certainly contact you if there are any negative inquiries or damages reported to my office." Cora extended her hand to shake, and Walter rose from his seat.

"Thank you, Mayor. I look forward to staying in touch and working together." Walter reached for Cora's offered hand and rotated her hand to hold it softly rather than return a business handshake. "Perhaps I could take you to dinner some evening. I could certainly use some help learning the locations of the popular restaurants. I am struggling on my own to get by. I must confess I am not much of a cook."

"We are very fortunate to have several choices in Spicetown and they all will offer you a delightful meal. You will not suffer for lack of cooking skills." Cora smiled as she walked toward her office door, willing Walter to swiftly follow. "It was a pleasure meeting you and best of luck in your endeavors."

"The pleasure was all mine." Walter reached for Cora's hand again, but she moved behind the door and grabbed the doorknob to avoid acknowledging it. What had started out as a peaceful encounter had turned tense and disturbing somewhere. She wasn't sure of the source of the anxiety but welcomed its departure.

"Miss Morgan," Walter nodded. "A pleasure."

"Have a good day, Mr. Slope."

"Indeed, it has already begun."

Cora Mae watched until Walter cleared the lobby

front entrance door and then turned toward Amanda with her hands on her hips. "I don't quite know what to make of all that just yet."

Chapter 2

"Can I take your order?" The waitress at the Caraway Cafe clicked the end of her ink pen and smiled as Peggy Cochran's head bobbed up.

"Hello, Amber. Can you get me two of today's special to go? It's too busy to leave the store for long so Arlene and I will have to eat between customers."

"Anything to drink?"

"No thanks. I've got drinks at the store. Is Dot in the kitchen?" Peggy sat up tall in her chair trying to peer through the open order window.

"Yes, she's back there. Do you need to see her?"

"Yes, if you'd let her know I'm out here, I'd like to talk to her if I can. It's not urgent if she's busy though. I can call her later if I need to."

"I'll tell her! Thanks." Amber slipped the menu off the table and tucked it into the stand near the door.

Peggy pulled her phone from her coat pocket and glanced at her email, opening the email she received from Grace Keslar that morning.

"Hey, Peg!" Dorothy Parish slid into the chair

opposite Peggy Cochran and propped her chin in the palm of her hand. "I could sure use a minute off my feet. How's business today?"

"It's busy today." Peggy nodded. "It's been busy since Thanksgiving. A lot of people are crafting this year and those quilt classes have really taken off. Having those weekend highlights at the community center on different kinds of art and do it yourself projects that Cora has been running has sure pumped up my business. Thank goodness I've got Arlene working full time with me now."

"I wish I could find some good help. I've needed another cook for months, but I just can't find one. I'm hoping things change after the holidays. Frank and I are worn thin."

"I guess we shouldn't complain about our businesses doing well." Peggy chuckled.

"True."

"But the reason I wanted to catch you was to ask if you knew about Grace Keslar's Christmas party. She stopped in the store yesterday and told me about it, but today I got an emailed invitation."

"I know about it." Dorothy huffed. "Who do you think is doing all the food? It's going to be a working event for me, I think."

"She told me about the bed and breakfast idea. She plans to let people stay in her house! I was shocked that she would do that. She asked me if she could advertise my business in her bed and breakfast promotion. She wants to offer her spa customers the opportunity to learn to knit, crochet, or sew."

"What? No, I didn't know about anything other than a Christmas party. That was shocking enough. Grace has been a recluse ever since she moved here, but it's been worse since her husband died. I can't believe she's inviting people to her home at all."

"Oh, she's been working on coming out of her shell. She started taking knitting classes from me this summer and comes in the store every week now. She wants to be a part of the community, but this party is actually to celebrate her new business venture."

"The bed and breakfast?"

"That's just a side business for her real project!" Peggy held her hands out with her palms up. "She's opening a wellness center."

"A what?" Dorothy glanced around the room when she realized her outburst turned a few heads and quieted her voice. "What's a wellness center?"

Peggy chuckled. "It's like a spa and a gym combined. They do spin class and meditation with massages and stuff like that." Peggy shrugged. "She plans to advertise all across the nation and when people come from far away to stay at the retreat, she will put them up overnight at her house."

"The bed and breakfast!" Dorothy pointed her finger at Peggy and smiled.

"Exactly. I have to admit, she's thought of everything. I'm just not sure people around here will be interested."

"The invitation I saw didn't say anything about a business opening. I thought it was just for Christmas. I'm making finger foods and festive holiday hors d'oeuvres. It's not a sit-down dinner, but I think Vicki Garwin is making her a Christmas tree cake. She hired Spicetown Blooms & Gifts to decorate. She's got the whole town involved."

Peggy laughed. "She's a sly one. No one will want to miss this party. The whole town has always been curious about her and her house. They won't want to miss it. Then when she has everyone's attention, she can make the announcement about the spa and inn opening on January 2nd."

"I bet she's doing that for tax purposes." Dorothy chuckled. "I need to get her to join our merchant association so she can teach us master business classes!"

"Thank you." Peggy handed her credit card to Amber when she placed a brown bag on the table. "I wonder if Gretchen and Levi know about all this."

Dorothy looked up and frowned. "There's room in this town for another bed and breakfast. The Nutmeg Inn is booked solid around the holidays. They'll be fine. If Grace can bring more people to Spicetown with her new idea, we will all benefit."

"Spoken like a true merchants association president!" Peggy squeezed Dorothy's forearm, and they both laughed too loudly as she snatched the bag off the table, waving as she pushed through the front doors to leave.

Dorothy straightened the table and walked over to the order window to peer across the grill. "Frank?"

Frank slid a plate on the counter and hit the bell for Amber to come pick it up.

"Frank, I need to run across the street for a minute and see Vicki."

"Right now?" Frank frowned. "What's so important?"

"New developments on the holiday front! I'll fill you in later. Be back in a jiff."

Frank rolled his eyes and chuckled. "Go on, then."

§

"Imogene!" Grace Keslar scooted through her dining room sliding her house slippers smoothly across the floor, so her cat, Chauncey, could chase her feet while she walked. For an octogenarian, she was still quite nimble from her many years of ballet.

"Imogene, do you know where Stanley went? The car is gone, and I don't remember sending him anywhere." Grace pushed open the swinging kitchen door as Imogene glanced over her shoulder. "Maybe I did send him somewhere. Did I tell him yesterday that I needed him to do something this morning? You know I can't remember all those details from one day to the next."

"Good morning, Miss Grace." Imogene chuckled and turned back toward the sink. "Stanley took those packages you wanted shipped out. I got everything boxed up this morning. Do you need him? I can give him a call."

"I wanted to go into town later and just wanted to make certain he was free. It's not urgent. I'm not even ready to go myself yet." Grace held her arms out to show she was still in her lounging suit and slippers.

"Oh, sure. He'll be back shortly."

"I'd like to go into town a bit later today. Maybe I could stop in the Nutmeg Inn. I've never been there."

"The Inn? Levi and Gretchen Nauchtman run the Nutmeg Inn. Have you met them before?"

Grace flapped her hands in the air. "I don't remember. Do you think I have? I might have. Chancellor may have invited them to the house a time or two. There were always so many people here at Christmas time and I could never remember any of them the next day."

"Are you going to invite them to your Christmas party?"

"Yes! Everyone is invited! The whole town can come if they like, don't you think? Don't you think that's a grand idea? Maybe I could just put an invitation in the newspaper, so everyone would know. Should I do that?" Grace looked down at her cat, Chauncey. "What do you think Master Keslar? If you could talk, I'm sure you would tell me to call the whole thing off."

Imogene turned around, drying her hands on a dish towel, and glared at the cat. "You know he'll be angry at you for weeks over this."

Grace shook her fluffy slippers under Chancey's nose until he couldn't resist slapping her shoe with his paw. "We can only hope he hides until it's over. If he decides to participate, it could get crazy in here."

Imogene laughed. "I think it will be crazy enough without a cat. I have to admit, I'm a little nervous about it. It will be strange having a party without Mr. K. He always set the tone for the gatherings. Does that make sense?"

Grace closed her eyes briefly and sighed. Chancellor Keslar was an intimidating man, but everyone respected him. He had been gone for eight years now and Grace was finally trying to live again. "I do. Ouch!" Grace lifted her foot in the air. "Take it easy, buddy. He bit my toe!"

Imogene giggled and shook her towel in Chauncey's face. Jumping at the towel, Imogene twirled it around until he flopped on his back to grab it with all four paws. "Now he has a new toy. That should occupy him for a couple of minutes."

“I guess inviting the whole town isn’t a great idea, but I do think I need to include all the business owners. Peggy Cochran told me she’s in a merchant’s association so I’m going to see if I can join that. Are the owners of the Nutmeg Inn nice people? I could stop in today and introduce myself.”

“They may see you as competition.” Imogene grimaced. “You may not get a warm welcome. You are opening a competing bed and breakfast.”

“Nonsense! Their business is for friends and family passing through the community. Mine is strictly to house guests at the spa. Surely, they won’t view it as a threat. I’ll be certain and explain that to them. I don’t want them to think I am trying to take away from their profits.”

Imogene shrugged. “It’s their livelihood and people get testy about those things. Do you think we should hire security for the party?”

Grace turned to leave, and Chauncey jumped up to follow. “That’s not necessary. I’ve invited the entire police force so that is all taken care of!”

Imogene shook her head and laughed as Grace pushed through the kitchen door.

Sheri Richey

Chapter 3

Marmalade Magnolia Bingham stomped into the middle of the kitchen, swished her fluffy orange tail, and meowed as loudly as she could just as Cora Mae transferred the green beans from the stove to the counter. "Now, what is that all about? Have we got company?"

Marmalade may be aging, but she still had acute hearing. She knew precisely when Police Chief Conrad Harris' car stopped in their driveway. Drying her hands, Cora headed for the front foyer and pulled the door open before Conrad's knuckles could rap.

"Evening," Conrad barked as Cora pushed the screen door open.

"Come on in. I was just putting it on the table." Cora turned and shuffled down the hall. "I just need to make the drinks."

Conrad slipped off his coat and scratched Marmalade on the head when she hollered up a hello. "Sorry I missed you Friday. Amanda said you left early," Conrad said as he walked into the kitchen.

"Yes, I left an hour early and ran over to Paxton. I

had a gift to pick up for my Sunday school class this morning. Today was Gerald Hawkins' last class. He and his wife are moving to Tennessee next week. They've been our class leaders for over ten years so everyone wanted to chip in and get them something nice to remember us by. I had to special order it, so it wasn't ready until Friday."

"I was just calling to see if you wanted to meet for dinner. It was weird day." Conrad chuckled as he pulled out a chair at the table.

"It was!" Cora Mae sat down across from Conrad and handed him a basket of dinner rolls. "I had an unusual visitor, and I didn't know quite what to make of it."

"Maybe we have the same story." Conrad smirked. "We had an odd visitor at the station, too. You go first."

"Well, Saucy came by and gave me an update on the Christmas play. He got another part with lines again, but there's something funny going on with it. I don't know what he's got up his sleeve this time. That's not the odd part though." Cora reached for her teacup and took a sip. "While we were chatting, he saw another cast mate in the lobby, so he brought him into the office to introduce. The man's name was Walter Slope, and he's the new mine manager."

"I didn't know the old one was gone." Conrad shrugged and reached for the saltshaker. "Was there something odd about the guy?"

"He said he had planned to come by and introduce himself. He wanted to talk to me and then he gave me a blast notice. They are going to close some tunnels down, so they have a series of blasting planned out on the north road."

“That’s just great.” Conrad huffed. “We’re going to have complaints from everybody in the new subdivision and out at the lake. I don’t think they’ve done any blasting up there since the subdivision was built.”

“I know it’s difficult.”

“I hope with the tunnels closing, that means there won’t be any more action in these areas in the future. It always puts me in an impossible position. Citizens call the office, and we tell them it’s the mine. They yell at us because they don’t have anybody else to take it out on.”

“He indicated the mine is in financial straits and he is here to save the place, to keep it from closing. The tunnel work is being done to cut operating costs. Something about him, gives me pause.”

“You don’t believe his story?” Conrad slapped butter on his dinner roll. “Is he giving you a bad vibe?”

“I think he’s trying to tell me what he thinks I want to hear. I couldn’t decide whether to be insulted or flattered.”

Conrad chuckled.

“I just didn’t know what to think of him, but I’d say he’s one to watch.” Cora pointed her index finger at Conrad before taking her next bite.

“Following along in the category of unusual behavior, Grace Keslar came into the Spicetown Police Department spreading holiday cheer.” Conrad tossed his hands up in the air.

“You know Grace,” Cora said, pointing with her fork. “You went to her house years ago when her husband had parties. She’s just stayed cooped up these last few years since he passed away. I saw her a few months ago in the Carom Seed Craft Corner. She's taking knitting lessons from Peggy and wanting to start getting involved in the community again."

"She's getting involved all right." Conrad shook his head. "She's having a Christmas party at the mansion and has invited every single one of my officers. I think she would have invited the folks in the cells if they hadn't all been empty."

Cora laughed. "It sounds like she is coming out of her shell."

"She has the holiday spirit."

"I haven't gotten an invitation yet, but I haven't seen her come in City Hall."

"Well, consider yourself invited." Conrad wiped his hands off and put his napkin in his plate. "You can be my plus one."

"Thank you." Cora Mae chuckled. "I don't feel so neglected now."

Conrad pulled his cell phone from his pocket and glanced at the display. "It's dispatch."

Cora waved dismissively. "Take it."

"Chief Harris..." Conrad rose from the table and wandered into the living room.

Cora Mae cleared the table and loaded the dishwasher while Conrad made a series of calls.

Conrad walked back into the kitchen and hiked up his pants before slipping his phone back in his pocket. "Well, I think I'm going to have a long night."

"Do you have to go to the station?"

"Yeah, and then I'm headed to the woods. The Sheriff's Office called and asked for an assist. They want Briscoe."

"Briscoe?"

"They've got a lost girl and they want help

searching. I've got to go home and wake up the boss." Conrad laughed. "I'm sure Briscoe is sawing logs right now."

Cora Mae smiled. "Is Briscoe a morning dog?"

"Yes, very much so. He does love a good walk in the woods though. I just haven't tried it at night." Conrad reached for his jacket. "Dinner was delicious. Thank you."

"You're welcome, anytime. Just be careful out there. You'll break your neck walking around in the dark."

"At least Briscoe won't let me get lost. I'll call you tomorrow."

§

"Who was on the phone?" Olivia D'Asaro popped a French fry into her mouth and dusted the salt from her fingers before reaching for her drink.

"The Sheriff's office!" Peter Jessup grabbed his shoes from under the coffee table and slipped them on. "I've got to get home. They think I'm there now and they want something of Jane's."

"Why?"

"They thought I called them. Apparently, somebody called and reported Jane was missing."

"Well, is she? When did you see her last?" Olivia dropped down on the couch next to Peter.

"I don't know. I saw her this morning." Peter shrugged. "I left early. I don't know where she is. She usually goes for a walk, takes pictures, things like that. I don't know. We don't really talk."

"Wow. Maybe she left town! That would be so great."

"Yeah, but she'd never make it that easy for me. She's probably done something crazy and now I've got the law on my back."

Peter slipped his coat on, and Olivia jumped up from the couch. Wrapping her arms around his neck, she gave Peter a quick kiss. "Call and let me know what's going on."

"I will, once I get all this stuff worked out. Who could have reported my wife missing? This is weird." Peter zipped up his coat just as his cell phone chimed with a text.

"Is that her?" Olivia followed Peter to the door.

"No, it's my mom. She's asking if I know where Jane is." Peter typed a response.

"Maybe the police called her, too." Oliva tugged on Peter's jacket. "If Jane's gone, you should come back here tonight. No reason to go home to an empty house."

Peter shook his head and reached for the door. "I've got to get to the house. I need to get there before they show up. I'll call you." Peter turned back and kissed her quickly before running outside to his car.

Chapter 4

"Evening, Chief." Sergeant Cantrell greeted Conrad with an extended hand once Briscoe's leash had been secured. "The sheriff's office appreciates your offering to help us tonight. We're working on getting a helicopter in the air with a search light, but our canines are not search and rescue trained."

Conrad shook his hand and adjusted the neck of his coat to block out the chilly wind. "I don't know how much success we can expect in the dark. Any leads on her location?"

"All we know is her friend told us she walks in this area every Sunday morning. Photography is a hobby of hers and he said she usually walks up toward the mine fence and around this side of the hill. It's fairly close to home for her."

"Is this friend your reporting party?" Conrad reached into his pockets and slipped on his leather gloves.

"He is. Trevor Mason. Do you know him? I think he lives in Spicetown."

"I do. He works at the Paxton coal mine. What's

his connection to the missing woman?"

"He said she's a friend."

Conrad scowled. "Trevor has a wife and young daughter at home on Lemon Lane. He lives next door to his in-laws." Conrad raised one eyebrow. "Is his wife out here with him reporting this?"

"No, Chief. He didn't mention a wife."

Conrad huffed. "Well, there's another chapter to that book. Got an article of clothing or something on your missing girl?"

"Sure do." Sergeant Cantrell walked over to his squad car and picked up a clear plastic bag with fabric inside. "Her husband is supposed to be bringing us something from home, too."

"Are we certain she came out here? I mean, did Trevor say he knew—"

"Yeah, Chief. He said he talked to her early this morning and invited her to attend church with him. She told him then that she planned to come out here instead. Trevor said he knew her phone didn't work in this area, but he had always asked her to text him when she returned home, so he wouldn't worry about her. Today, she never sent him a text."

Conrad pulled the floral material from the bag and offered it to Briscoe. Handing the bag back to Sergeant Cantrell, Conrad responded to the tug Briscoe gave him and aimed the flashlight to offer him the best view.

Briscoe began by sweeping the area left to right looking for a scent. Briscoe had previously proven himself as a people finder, locating the dead and still alive, and apparently word had gotten out about it. He had never talked to the sheriff's office about his pet, turned officer. He was conflicted with the recognition. He naturally wanted to be of help where needed, but he didn't want Sheriff Bell treating him as his own personal tool. On the other hand, he would enjoy showing Bobby Bell that they could find the missing girl when his staff could not. He had no doubt that Briscoe would find the young woman, if she was out here.

Conrad glanced over his shoulder and saw Sergeant Cantrell jogging around in the dark trying to keep up with him. "Do you need a light?"

"No, I've got it." Sergeant Cantrell flipped on a small flashlight and began to step lighter. "Sorry. You took off faster than I expected."

Conrad chuckled. "Briscoe is in charge. I'm just following."

"When my deputies get here, they should have something to offer a better scent. Mr. Mason said that jacket belonged to Mrs. Jessup, but she hasn't worn it in a week or so."

Conrad nodded.

"I thought I'd follow along with you, so we'll get the radio notice to go back once they show up."

Conrad unzipped his jacket a few inches when he began to overheat. Briscoe had committed to a route which hastened his steps but took them away from the light. "I guess we're going this way off to the left now. Do you think you could get them to pull some lighting around this way?"

Sergeant Cantrell issued directives by radio and then stopped at the response he received. "Do you want to go back and wait to see if the clothing they bring will be better?"

"Can't stop now. I don't want to interrupt him. You go on back," Conrad yelled as they moved farther away from Sergeant Cantrell. “We’ll be fine.”

Conrad could not interpret what Sergeant Cantrell said next but widened the beam on his hand-held light and slipped on a headlamp that he had pocketed before he left the station.

“I hope you know what you’re doing,” Conrad said to Briscoe once they were alone. “I hope you’re not out here running around because it’s fun. I’m already worn out, and it’s past my bedtime!”

Conrad groaned when Briscoe didn’t acknowledge him. It was a sure sign that Briscoe was on a mission and his past missions had usually turned out badly for someone involved.

§

“We appreciate it, Mr. Jessup. Take all the time you need. We’ll wait right here for you.” Deputy Joshua Pate glanced at Deputy Lisa McWhorter and rolled his eyes.

“What would be the best choice?” Peter Jessup hollered down the hallway from the door to his wife’s bedroom. “Any certain kind of thing?”

“Something she wore recently is best. Maybe what she slept in last night or wore yesterday would be the best choice.” Deputy Pate turned down the radio on his belt as Deputy McWhorter pointed down the hallway.

“Did you hear that?” she whispered.

Pate shook his head and squinted to see if that would help his hearing. “What?”

“He just said he doesn’t know what she wore.” Deputy McWhorter’s eyebrows arched. Raising her voice, she yelled down the hallway, “Can I be of any help to you, Mr. Jessup?"

"No. No, I got this." Peter Jessup came wandering slowly out of the bedroom holding several different articles of clothing. "I got this t-shirt that I think she slept in last night. This other shirt was on the floor, so I bet she wore it yesterday."

"I think either will work nicely for what we need," Deputy McWhorter said reaching for the clothing.

"I also found this towel on the bathroom floor. I guess she used it this morning when she showered."

Deputy Pate shook his head. "I think the shirts are the best option."

Peter Jessup nodded and watched Deputy McWhorter bag each of the items. "Okay," he said as he shuffled back and forth on each foot, looking up and then around the room. "So, what now? What am I supposed to do?" Peter paced over toward the couch as if he planned to sit, then turned around and paced back.

"We'd like for you to come with us, if you can. You might be able to help us with the search."

"Yeah! Oh, yeah. That's good. I can do that. No problem." Peter zipped up his coat. "Let's go! Should I drive?"

"No, sir. We'll give you a lift." Deputy McWhorter patted Peter on the back as they walked toward the car. Opening the back door, she waited for him to climb inside before she got in the front seat.

When Deputy Pate started the car, Deputy McWhorter turned around in her seat. "Mr. Jessup, do you remember what time your wife left this morning?"

"No, ma'am. I left before she did."

"Did she tell you where she was going this

morning?"

"No, but if the weather is nice, she usually does go walking in the woods on Sunday morning. She says the morning light is the best time to take pictures."

"She's a photographer?" Deputy McWhorter glanced at Joshua Pate.

"It's mostly a hobby, but she has sold some of them. She'd like to do it full-time."

"When does she usually get home on the days she goes walking in the woods?"

"Uh, I don't know. It's different all the time. Maybe noon." Peter shrugged.

"Did you hear from her at all today?" Deputy Pate said as he glanced into the rear-view mirror. "Did she call you?"

"No."

"So, you didn't know anything was wrong." Deputy McWhorter peeked around the headrest.

Peter just shook his head.

"The area that we're currently searching is about half a mile from your house. Is that the area she usually goes? Would your wife have driven her car there this morning? We haven't found a car."

"No, she walked. Her car is at the house. In the summer, sometimes she'll take her bicycle, but not when it's cold. If one of the neighbors was heading out of the subdivision, they might have given her a lift and dropped her off."

Lisa McWhorter whipped around in her seat. "Ah! Well, maybe we need to canvas your neighbors. That might give us a better starting spot."

"I could make a few calls..." Peter pulled his phone out of his pocket and looked through his contacts.

"You must have some pretty great neighbors."

Deputy Pate glanced in the mirror again and chuckled. "I don't even know mine and I've lived in Paxton for five years."

"Well, we all work together, so everybody knows everybody else."

"Your neighbors work with you?" Deputy McWhorter frowned.

"Most everyone in the subdivision works for the mine. Nobody else would want to live out here in the middle of nowhere, but we love it because we're just minutes from work. Everybody calls it Miner's Meadow, but the real name is Millet Meadows." Peter shrugged. "Anybody would have given her a lift if they'd seen her, I think."

Deputy Pate pulled his squad car over on the side of the road and parked.

"I'll let the Sergeant know we're back and get this to him." Lisa held up the bag. "I'll see where he wants us."

Deputy Pate nodded. "We can just wait here until she gets back. I'm going to write up what you've told us so far, in case the Sergeant needs the information. Is there anything you can think of that might help us locate your wife?"

Peter Jessup was leaning forward and peering out the side window of the squad car. "Hmm? Uh, no."

"Mr. Jessup, did you notice anything different or off at the house? Were her personal items still in the normal place, like her toothbrush, her shoes, her clothes? Did everything seem normal?"

"Yeah, I guess."

"Are we certain that she didn't just decide to leave—?"

"No, she wouldn't just leave like that!" Peter held

both hands open in front of him and raised his voice. “It’s not like that.”

“Okay.” Deputy Pate held up his hand to stop the emotional flow. “I’m just trying to look at all angles. Does she ever take a friend with her? Or call anyone when she’s out walking? Like a girlfriend or family member?”

“No, the cell service is awful on that side of the hill. She always said her coverage was spotty there. I don’t think she ever called anyone when she was walking. She never said anything about it.”

“Okay,” Deputy Pate adjusted his mirror, so he didn’t have to turn around. “Do you have any idea what could have happened to her?”

“No! She’s got to be out there somewhere! There’s no other answer.”

“We’ve been searching since six o’clock this evening. We’ve requested a helicopter with search lights. There is a team of officers and a canine searching. We just need to be certain we’re looking in the right place. That’s a lot of resources to be targeting the wrong spot.”

“Yeah, yeah. I get it.”

“Maybe you could try calling a neighbor or two. See if anyone saw her walking this morning or maybe gave her a lift. That might help us pin down a location.”

“I can do that.” Peter looked at his phone again.

“Does your wife have any enemies? Any neighbor that she doesn’t get along with?”

“You think somebody kidnapped her?” Peter smirked and then smiled into the rear-view mirror. “Nah, everybody likes Jane. Me, not so much, but they all think she’s a gem.”

Chapter 5

"Good morning, Ms. Morgan." Walter Slope sauntered into Amanda's office and smiled. "Would it be possible for me to speak with the mayor for just a second? I promise I won't keep her. Just a quick question and I'll be out of your way."

"Well," Amanda glanced at the phone and sighed. "I think she's on the phone right now. If you want to take a seat, I'll check with her."

Walter mouthed the words, "Thank you," without a sound, stuck a toothpick in his mouth, and turned to find a chair against the wall. Amanda slipped herself quietly into Cora Mae's office and even more quietly shut the door.

Cora barely acknowledged Amanda, assuming she was coming in to do some filing, and continued typing her email until Amanda cleared her throat.

Cora looked up, wide-eyed and quizzical, and then turned her chair towards Amanda.

"Walter Slope is in my office," Amanda whispered. "I know you said you didn't— Well, you weren't too crazy about—. I didn't know if you'd really want to see him or not. I can tell him you're too busy, if you want."

Cora scrunched her nose up and puckered her lips. "I didn't think he'd really come back." Cora sighed. "I guess you should just let him in. If it's not today, it won't go away."

Amanda took a deep breath and slipped back out into her outer office, leaving Cora's office door open.

"Mr. Slope. You can go in now. She has a couple of minutes before her meeting."

Cora smiled at Amanda's impromptu setup. "Thank you, dear." Walking around her desk, she waited for Mr. Slope to appear at the door.

"Please have a seat, Mr. Slope. How can I help you today?" Cora motioned him in and returned to her desk chair.

"Good morning, Mayor. It's a pleasure to see you again."

Cora Mae forced a smile but couldn't find any words.

"I promised Ms. Morgan I would only be a minute. I just wanted to stop in and ask you if you were free for lunch today. I'm in town all morning and have meetings to attend to myself, but I'd like to find a nice place downtown for lunch. I thought perhaps you could accompany me. I could use your guidance. As I mentioned last week, I still have much to explore and am lost as to where to begin."

Cora sat frozen, but behind her blank stare, she turned several scenarios over in her mind. Conrad could join them. She frequently had lunch with him, and it would be more comfortable that way.

"I'm sure we can arrange something. I usually eat downtown on Mondays. We may have other community members join us, but it will give you a chance to meet some other people around town."

"Delightful," Walter said as he rose from his chair.

"Why don't you come back by around noon, and we'll walk down the street for a bite."

"I will be here!"

Amanda appeared at the door. "Excuse me, Mayor. I'm—"

"I'll get out of your way." Walter passed by Amanda. "See you at noon." Walter wiggled his fingers in goodbye as he walked out of the door and Amanda looked at Cora Mae.

"I'm sorry. I got in here as soon as I realized what was happening." Amanda's brow furrowed.

"It's okay, dear. I'll just call the Chief and have him meet us at the Caraway Cafe." Cora nodded. "I think he means well, and I feel sorry for him. Being new in town and not knowing anyone except your employees. He can't very well socialize with them, and he has to start somewhere. I just got an uncomfortable vibe from him last week. I don't know why. We just got off on the wrong foot."

"I don't know, Mayor." Amanda shook her head. "I'm a believer in first impressions, especially when they're yours."

Cora Mae laughed. "Let me call the Chief and give him a heads up." Cora reached for the phone and hit her speed dial for the Spicetown Police Department, waiting for Dispatcher Georgia Marks to give the standard greeting. "Georgie, is the Chief in?"

Amanda bowed out of the office and pulled the door shut.

"Sorry, Mayor. He's out in the woods with Briscoe looking for the lost girl. I don't think his cell phone is working out there, but he may be back shortly. Officer Kimball just headed that way to relieve him. Do you want me to have him call when he comes in?"

"Yes. It's not urgent. I was just calling to tell him that there is a luncheon today with the new mine manager at the Caraway Cafe. If he's free, please tell him we'd love to have him. If not, I understand."

"I sure will!"

"Thank you, Georgia." Cora pushed her chair back and walked around her desk. Opening her office door, she waved Amanda back in her office.

Amanda took a seat across from Cora's desk with her pad in her hand.

"I struck out." Cora's brow furrowed. "The Chief is helping the Sheriff's office with a missing person case. I don't know that he will be able to join me for lunch."

"Oh, yeah! Brian told me all about it. He knows Jane Jessup. They were friends in high school, and he knows her husband, too. I think they were both in his class."

"I didn't know who was involved. I thought it was a girl from Paxton. I don't think I know anyone named Jane Jessup." Cora Mae wrote the name on her desk pad and stared at it.

"She was Jane Platt in school, but I don't think she moved here until high school. She married Peter Jessup."

"I had a student named Paul Jessup—"

"That's his brother," Amanda said, holding her finger up. "I think he was older than Peter."

"All I remember about Paul is that he had a very demanding mother. She was always sending me notes or dropping by after class to criticize me for one thing or another. When the school year ended, she told the principal that she didn't want her other children to be in my class. I thanked the principal for that good news." Cora Mae laughed. "I felt blessed."

"I know who Jane is, but I can't say I know her. Bryan introduced me to Peter when he came by the nursery one day. He seemed like a nice guy, but Bryan said their marriage has problems. He thought maybe she just left him, not got lost in the woods at all. She's a nature hiker and goes out there alone all the time."

"Georgia said they're still looking. The Chief is out there with Briscoe."

"Bryan said there was a helicopter looking last night. He heard it. Maybe somebody saw her, and they know she was out there." Amanda shrugged. "I just can't see her getting lost."

"I suppose something could have happened to her while she was walking. Maybe she hurt herself. Georgia said there is no cell service in the area they are searching. Maybe she couldn't call for help."

"Bryan was telling me that they are really struggling as a couple. He likes them both, but they haven't been really together for quite a while. He thinks they stay together because Peter's mother wouldn't approve of divorce. They are just living separate lives."

"I can't imagine either of them is happy that way." Cora Mae shook her head. "Speaking of getting married, are you getting cold feet?"

Amanda smiled. "No, not at all. I'm a little anxious about the wedding, but I've really surprised myself with the choices I've made."

"What do you mean?"

"I always thought I wanted a big wedding. I wanted ten bridesmaids because I didn't want to leave out any of my friends. I wanted a big party at the reception with a live band and I wanted to go to a tropical island for a honeymoon." Amanda waved her arms in the air. "The bigger the better."

"And you don't want that now?" Cora Mae shook her head.

"No way! I can't imagine doing any of that now. It just sounds crazy to me. I guess I've changed a lot. I just want something simple and pretty. I want a pleasant day to remember, not a wild bash."

"I think that sounds lovely." Cora smiled. "I know it will be a wonderful day for you both."

"If it's okay, I'd like to leave a little early tomorrow. I made an appointment at the Fennel Street Bakery to taste some cake samples. They are only open until four o'clock, so I couldn't get in after work."

"Of course, dear. That will be fine. Is your mother going with you?"

Amanda's head jerked back and the space between her eyebrows folded up like an accordion. "No. Bryan is going to come to town and meet me. Mavis is going to watch the store for him."

"Oh, I thought maybe your mother was helping you with wedding arrangements." Cora glanced out of her office window and waited to see if Amanda would address this elephant in the room. Since Bryan and Amanda had announced their intent to marry, Amanda had not mentioned her mother at all. Although their relationship had always been strained, Cora had hoped the event might draw them together with a common goal.

"No," Amanda said with a bowed head. "My

mother isn't interested, but really, I think it's for the best. We rarely see eye to eye on anything. Trying to work with her would probably be disastrous. She's such a strong personality that the wedding would become what she wanted, rather than my vision."

"I can see that," Cora conceded. "Men are not usually much help with these things, but your father will definitely do his part when called upon. He seems very happy."

A smiled bloomed on Amanda's face and she nodded. "Dad is the best."

"And I'm always here for you, dear. I'm just an old lady, but I sure do have opinions, so call on me if you need a consult!" Cora Mae laughed.

Amanda chuckled and smiled. "I definitely will! Thank you."

Sheri Richey

Chapter 6

"Hey, Kimball." Conrad nodded over his shoulder when he saw Officer Gwen Kimball approach.

"I'm here to relieve you, Chief. Georgia told me what's going on. Did you get any sleep last night?"

"Yeah, we quit at midnight. We were cold and tired. The helicopter got here around one o'clock, but the deputies stayed through the night. Briscoe and I didn't start back at it until a little after six this morning."

"How long are we going to keep covering the same ground? Do we even know for sure she was here?"

"We do. Briscoe found her camera first thing this morning. We know she was here."

"Wow. Okay, so where does that leave us?" Officer Kimball pulled on her leather gloves.

"The camera was found up the hill near the back fence line of the mine. I started there and I've been walking down. I'm thinking maybe she fell, rolled down the hill..." Conrad shrugged. "Once I hit the clearing, I go back up and fan out a different direction.

Briscoe isn't getting any scent so far today."

"Sergeant Cantrell gave me this." Gwen handed a plastic bag to Conrad. "He said her friend brought it to him. It looks like a coat. He thought it might have a better scent."

"Some guy named Trevor?" Conrad squinted.

"Yeah, Chief. He's down there with Cantrell."

"He identified the camera. I don't know where the husband went. They were going to canvas the residents in Miner's Meadow to see if anyone saw her walking yesterday. The friend seems to know more about what's going on than anyone else."

Conrad pulled the coat out of the bag and held it in front of Briscoe while Gwen took charge of the leash.

"Use your radio if you need anything. The cell service out here is sketchy. Call in to Georgia if you find anything."

"Will do, Chief." Gwen pushed the coat back in the bag and let Briscoe pull her east through the trees and away from the path.

Once he came out of the trees, Conrad searched the command station for a thermos of coffee but found nothing. Heading for his car, he waved at Sergeant Cantrell.

"Heading out, Chief?" Sergent Cantrell held a clipboard close to his chest and walked toward Conrad's squad car.

"Yeah, Officer Kimball is going to take over for a bit. I'm going to warm up."

"We may need to talk to a few people today. Would it be okay to bring them to the PD? Your office is a lot closer than driving them to Paxton."

"Sure. That's not a problem. Have you talked to the husband and this friend?" Conrad smirked when he looked over at Trevor Mason. "I can think of a few questions for them."

Sergeant Cantrell chuckled. "Yeah, my deputies tell me the husband is not much in touch with our missing girl. It may be a marriage in name only."

Conrad nodded. "Is somebody developing the film in the camera?"

"Yeah, I had a deputy drive that back to County. They'll get it developed today."

Conrad waved as he turned to open his car door. "Holler if you need me."

"Thanks, Chief."

Conrad slammed the car door and started the engine. He waited patiently for his heater to warm and checked his phone for a signal. Once he reached the street, he did have a weak signal and messages that had been delayed all morning began to populate.

Dispatcher Georgia Marks texted to tell him she was sending Officer Kimball to relieve him. Mayor Bingham invited him to lunch to meet the mine manager and Officer Tabor asked if his presence was needed for the search. Conrad replied to Georgia that he was headed to the office and pulled out on the blacktop road near the entrance to Miner's Meadow. Turning toward Spicetown, he flipped the heat controls wide open and prayed that someone in the office had made coffee.

§

"Lovely, Imogene." Grace Keslar walked a path in front of the three ladies, then turned and walked back again, glancing at each woman from head to toe. "I'm so happy to see Imogene has made wonderful selections. I hope you each are happy to be chosen because we are very happy to have you." Grace stopped and clasped her hands.

The three women quietly muttered and nodded, glancing at each other, and then at Imogene nervously.

"This is Melissa Udall," Imogene said as she pointed at the first woman standing to their left. Shorter than the others, Melissa was trying to hold her stomach in and stand up straight. "She has experience in personal housekeeping and—"

"You shall be Thumper," Grace said as she stood in front of Melissa, again looking her up and down. "You will be in charge of all the dusting!" Grace arched her arms out and rotated her body to indicate the entire building. "It's a big place, but I know you will do a wonderful job at it, my dear."

"Thank you." Melissa's eyes darted over to Imogene with a startled expression tinged with a tiny amount of fear.

"And who is this?" Grace looked at Imogene.

"This is Rosa Newberg. She has hotel experience and just recently moved back to Spicetown."

"Splendid!" Grace pressed her palms together and lifted her chin. "Quite tall. Hmm, I think you shall be Olive, although your hair is not very dark." Grace hummed and studied the short wavy bob of Rosa's light brown hair. "Yes," Grace said as she pointed at Rosa's feet. "You shall be Olive and you will handle all of the floors! We have three active floors and then there is the cellar. You will keep all the floors clean for us and follow Thumper to collect what she loses."

With a firm nod, Grace stepped in front of the third woman. "You have lovely hair, my child."

"This is Kassie Jackson," Imogene said. "This will be her first housekeeping job, but I will train her."

Grace smiled at Kassie, who smiled back warmly. Although younger than the others and perhaps inexperienced, she was uniquely comfortable with the scrutiny. "Can you make a bed?"

"Oh, yes, ma'am. I can do that." Kassie pushed her glasses up on her nose with her index finger.

"Delightful! You shall be Alice and in charge of all the beds in the house. There are many. I can't recall how many, but you will learn them all. Each room has a distinct personality and a different name. You will learn them all and keep the integrity of each of them intact."

"I will do that, Mrs. Keslar. Thank you." Kassie stood at attention with wide eyes.

"Please call me Mistral."

"Miss Straw?" Kassie said with a frown.

"Mistral!" Grace shouted.

"Miss Trawl?" Rosa asked timidly, glancing again at Imogene and hoping for some guidance.

"Yes! Mistral. Because I must be strong like the northwest wind off the south coast of France!" Grace then spun on her heel and left the dining room with a stiff back and a cool expression.

"Come on in the kitchen for a minute and have a seat. I'll go over some basic information with you before we tour the house." Imogene pushed open the swinging kitchen door and smiled.

Stanley held up a cup of coffee in greeting. "Morning, Ladies. Can I get you some coffee?"

"This is Stanley. He takes care of the grounds and drives Mrs. Keslar wherever she needs to go."

"Do you mean Miss Trawl?" Rosa raised an

eyebrow.

"Yes." Imogene gave Stanley a knowing smile. "Let me introduce you. This is Alice, Olive and Thumper."

"Do we really have to use those names?" Melissa huffed.

"You don't like Thumper?!" Stanley chuckled. "It's the little bunny rabbit in Bambi. I'd say it's quite the compliment."

"Really?" Melissa frowned. "I don't know..."

"Cute as a button, I'd say." Imogene patted Melissa's shoulder.

"It makes me feel fat." Melissa wrinkled her nose and pressed her hand on her stomach.

"Am I supposed to be Olive Oyl?" Rosa scowled when Melissa chuckled. "I don't find that very flattering."

"No, I don't think Mrs. Keslar is probably familiar with Popeye. She did not grow up in the United States. Her connection to names and places is very different from ours. You probably remind her of someone she knew in France." Imogene placed three cups on the table.

"So, we have to use these names when we work here?" Kassie reached for the carafe filled with orange juice and poured it into her coffee cup.

"Yes." Imogene nodded. "Once Mrs. Keslar names you, she will only call you by that name. It's actually a very good practice when you work in the public eye. Once we start having guests in the house, they will never know your real name and the anonymity gives you some protection."

"Yeah, I guess so," Kassie said. "I don't mind. So, I am supposed to call her Miss Trawl?"

"Yes, but she will answer to Mrs. Keslar also." Imogene poured coffee for Rosa and Melissa.

"So, she gave you the name Imogene?" Melissa reached for the sugar bowl.

"It is my given name," Imogene sighed. "I never used it before working here. My friends and family call me Millie, but at work I am Imogene."

"What's your real name, Stanley?" Rosa took a sip from her coffee.

"Donald." Stanley chuckled and leaned against the kitchen counter.

"She doesn't like that name?" Melissa protruded her bottom lip in a pout.

"Mrs. Keslar never likes to use the same name twice. She probably already knew a Donald, and she decided Stanley suited me. That was thirteen years ago."

"So, you guys don't call her Miss Trawl either? Is that her maiden name?" Kassie raised her eyebrows and glanced from Stanley to Imogene.

"I usually call her Mrs. K." Stanley frowned. "She gives herself different names sometimes depending on her mood or the setting."

"I've heard her use it before," Imogene said. "It's French for something." Waving her hand dismissively, Imogene took a seat at the table.

"Is Mrs. Keslar okay?" Melissa furrowed her brow and leaned forward. "I mean is she always a little crazy or what?"

"She's perfectly sane. Eccentric, perhaps, but perfectly sane. She just speaks what she thinks and never worries about what others expect. Don't underestimate her."

"Oh, I won't." Rosa shook her head vigorously,

still showing slight signs of fear.

"I like her," Kassie said. "I think it will be fun working for her."

Stanley chuckled. "Oh, it definitely is. Every day is a new adventure."

Imogene smiled and gave Stanley a furtive glance. "Now, let me explain the basic layout of the mansion."

"I'll see you ladies later." Stanley rinsed his coffee mug out at the sink and sat it on the counter. "Don't forget to warn them about the cat." Stanley chuckled as he pushed through the kitchen door.

Chapter 7

Walter Slope climbed the steps to the Nutmeg Inn and yanked the front door open. The welcome sign clanked against the window and a melody chimed in the empty lobby. Glancing from left to right, he saw overstuffed sofas, cozy rugs and a hot drink bar with cocoa, tea, and coffee, but not a single person.

Hearing noises from behind the swinging door behind the check-in desk, he tried to wait patiently, but his fingers itched to tap the bell on the counter.

"Oh! Good morning." Gretchen Nauchtman scurried over to the counter. "How can I help you?"

Walter pulled the toothpick from his mouth and turned on his winning smile. "Good morning! I'm Walter Slope, the new manager out at the Paxton Mine northeast of town."

"Nice to meet you," Gretchen said as she offered her hand for a timid shake. "I'm Gretchen. My husband and I own the Nutmeg Inn."

"Splendid! I wanted to stop in and see your establishment. You see, from time to time, my corporate management team needs to visit for a few days. In the past, they have always found lodgings in Paxton. The mine office is slightly closer to Spicetown though, and I think they would appreciate the lovely environment here. I was hoping you might be able to accommodate them for future visits."

"We would be happy to—" Gretchen's head jerked up as the front door opened. "How many rooms do they usually require?"

"Usually just a couple of rooms. It varies, but I'd like to offer them the option if you think you can accommodate them."

Grace Keslar stood behind Walter Slope and waved her gloved hand at Gretchen.

"I'll be with you in just a moment, ma'am." Gretchen reached under the counter and pulled out some brochures. "This has some photos and a pricing sheet. We also have a website that you can share with your visitors. Our establishment does get booked to capacity during some of Spicetown holiday events, but otherwise we should be able to accommodate your visitors, Mr. Slope."

"Perhaps I can offer some help here," Grace said as she stepped up to the counter next to Walter. "My name is Grace Keslar."

"It's nice to meet you. I'm Walter Slope."

"I just stopped by to let Gretchen and Levi know that after the first of the year, I will be opening my home to guests also. That might be helpful to you if your visitors can't be accommodated here."

"The mansion?" Gretchen's eyes bugged out. "You're letting people—"

"Yes, dear," Grace smiled at Gretchen. "I'm opening a new business, a natural spa, and I'm offering my home to provide lodging to the spa visitors."

Gretchen huffed. "Oh. So, you're not opening a bed and breakfast. You're only going to let people stay there that come to your spa?"

"Well, I wouldn't turn anyone away, but I wanted you to know that there would be additional lodging in case you find someone needing a room when you are full. Spicetown just keeps growing and becoming more popular all the time. I think we will need more lodging options to meet future demand."

"It's a wonderful little town," Walter said, hoping to break the tension. "Tell me about your spa! My visitors might be interested in those services as well."

Grace reached for Walter's arm and turned him toward the door. "I'd love to."

"Thank you," Walter called out over his shoulder to Gretchen as he let Mrs. Keslar pull him away.

"Call if you have any questions," Gretchen yelled over the door chime as they left. "The number is on the—"

Walter pulled the front door shut and took Mrs. Keslar's arm as she stepped down each of the front steps gingerly. Her car and driver waited at the street. "So, you live in a mansion? Here in Spicetown?"

Grace patted his arm. "I am just outside the city limits, but Spicetown is my home now. My husband built us a rather large house when we first moved here and the people in town call it a mansion." Grace chuckled. "My husband loved to entertain and kept the house full of friends and family when we were younger."

"So where is the spa?"

"Irenic Wellness is northeast of town, and it opens

after the holidays. We will offer restorative health and nutritional guidance. There will be many options for enhancing physical health, from spin class to yoga, and mental health through meditation and massage. It's a very well-rounded program; something for everyone!"

"It sounds wonderful." Walter glanced at the driver who was reaching for the car door.

"That is my goal!" Grace chuckled and stepped toward the opening car door. "Thank you."

"It was very nice to meet you, Mrs. Keslar. I am new to Spicetown myself. I am the new manager out at the Paxton mine."

"Oh! You see, the town is growing. I am having a Christmas party to celebrate my new business venture. You will come and meet the rest of Spicetown. Everyone will be there!"

"I would love to! Thank you."

Grace slipped into the car and wiggled her fingers goodbye through the window as Stanley ran around to the other side of the car.

Walter smiled and waved back as the car sped down Ginger Street. Pulling his phone from his coat pocket, he sent a quick text message. *I just met Grace Keslar completely by accident!*

"Is Jill expecting you?" Stanley asked Grace Keslar over his shoulder as he turned onto Paprika Parkway.

"Yes and no," Grace said with a giggle. "I didn't specifically tell her I was coming today, but I've told her she must always be prepared to expect me at any time. You know I don't like to map out my entire life into the square box of a schedule."

"Oh, I know, but I wasn't sure Jill knew that." Stanley smiled into the rear-view mirror. "Did she hire an assistant yet?"

"She has. I'm hoping the young woman will be there this morning so I can meet her. Jill said she hired her away from a gym in Paxton, where she was working as a personal trainer. Before that, she worked in one of those rock-climbing businesses up north. Do you think we need to put in a rock-climbing wall? That might be something different."

"Nah, we have plenty of natural hills around here if anyone wants to climb."

"Hmm, that's true." Grace frowned. "I hope Jill can get along with the young woman. Jill is very competent, but she can be a bit brusque. She needs someone to handle the customer service side of things, so she can focus on the efficiency of the business. I hope she selected someone that will fill that need."

"There are a lot of cars here." Stanley pulled into the parking lot of Irenic Wellness. "Looks like they got the sign up."

"Yes! It's looks nice. Jill said she hired some local labor to help her with some work around the facility. I guess that's why all the vehicles are here. Come inside with me. She might need your help, too."

Stanley nodded and parked near the front entrance. Helping Mrs. Keslar from the car, Stanley glanced at the glass doors and saw a young woman peering out. He smiled and pushed the car door closed. As he reached for the door handle, the young woman flipped the lock on the door and pointed to the sign.

Removing a blue candy cane from her mouth, she

yelled, "We're not open."

Stanley nodded and yelled back through the glass door. "This is Mrs. Keslar, the owner."

The young girl scowled and then glanced over her shoulder. Backing away, Stanley saw Jill coming across the lobby.

"I guess that's the new girl," Stanley shrugged. "Jill's coming."

Hearing the flip of the lock, Grace stepped back when the door opened.

"Mrs. Keslar! So sorry. We weren't expecting you. Come in." Grace walked in, ignoring the young girl, and looked around at the lobby. "The trim is not up."

Pointing at the ceiling, Jill looked up. "It's on our list. We have some little things to finish up. I have some guys in the back room putting down the baseboard trim now. They'll be in here next."

"I hired a young man to do evening spin classes for you today." Grace walked toward the room designated for yoga classes when she heard voices coming from the room. Glancing in the doorway, she watched two men cutting long lengths of quarter-round into measured pieces.

"Oh, really?" Jill glanced at Olivia. "That's good. This is Olivia D'Asaro, the young woman I hired as my assistant." Jill held her arm out toward the candy cane girl, but Grace did not acknowledge her.

"His name is Jason Marks, and he works at the Caraway Cafe during the day. He is experienced, and he has a delightful personality. He will be well-liked I think."

"Good." Jill cleared her throat.

"I told him to stop by on his day off and see you to do whatever paperwork you need from him."

"Okay. I'll keep an eye out for him."

Grace wandered from room to room, looking at each crevice and corner while Stanley, Jill and Olivia followed her in silence.

"Have you had any difficulties? Is there anything you need help with?" Grace stopped and spun around to face Jill.

"Um, there is an area on the back side of the building that we need to fill in with dirt or rock. There's a trench where water stands when it rains. I think they just forgot about it, but it needs some attention. Did you decide about landscaping on the front yet? I know it's hard to do this time of year, but—"

"I have thought about it." Grace pivoted quickly on her toes and headed back towards the entrance only to stop right inside the double doors. When she turned abruptly again, Jill and Olivia stepped back. "And we can discuss it another time."

"Yes, ma'am." Jill glanced at Stanley who averted his eyes.

Pushing the door open, Stanley held it open until Grace walked through to the outside door. Looking over his shoulder, he whispered, "Thanks. We'll see you later."

His words stopped Jill in her tracks, and she held up a hand to Olivia who opened her mouth to speak.

Grace climbed into the car and sat stoically until Stanley started the engine. After backing out of the parking place and pulling onto the blacktop road, he looked in the mirror. "Where to next, Mrs. K?"

"I think that will be enough for now. I'm sure Imogene is making something for lunch, and I need to think on a few things this afternoon."

Stanley nodded. “I guess you weren’t impressed by the new assistant.”

“You are not just guessing, Stanley.” Grace smiled, and the tension faded from her posture.

Over the many years Stanley had worked closely with Grace Keslar, he had learned she did not make judgments based on someone’s physical appearance. She actually felt a spiritual energy when she met someone new.

“She doesn’t give off the aura we need. I will have to look for someone more appropriate.”

Stanley nodded and smiled. “I think Ms. Imogene has some Brunswick Stew and cornbread planned for us today and that sounds mighty good to me.”

Grace cooed. “It does indeed.”

Chapter 8

Cora Mae bundled her neck scarf closer when a gust of wind kicked up. Walking down Fennel Street, she tucked her chin down and nodded as Walter Slope walked along beside her seemingly unaffected by the weather.

"I hope you've had a productive day today. It's been an amazing day for me. I've visited a number of different businesses this morning. Just trying to get my bearings in town and it has been a joy. Everyone has been so welcoming."

"That's good to hear." Cora Mae's muffled response was met with concern.

"The wind is quite chilly. Would you like for me to go back for the car?" Walter extended his arm behind Cora to pull her against him, but she stepped away and lifted her chin.

"No. No, I'm fine and we're very close. It was just a little gusty for a moment. I hope you'll find something you like at the Caraway Cafe. Dorothy and Frank Parrish have had a successful restaurant here for years. Dorothy is also the founder and president of our merchants association."

"Oh, I'm sure I will. I think I walked by there earlier today. I went to the bakery for breakfast and so I walked down Fennel Street. I'm staying just a block over on Tarragon Street right now."

"That will be handy."

"Yes, the company offered me a rental in Paxton, but this is closer, and I think I'd much prefer being in Spicetown."

"I find it much nicer, too," Cora chuckled. "I might be a tad bit biased though."

Walter opened the door to the Caraway Cafe and held it open for Cora.

Cora Mae began removing her coat and led Walter to the table in the front window. "I usually sit here. I like to people watch."

"Best seat in the house!" Walter hustled around the table to pull out a chair for Cora.

"Thank you." Cora Mae draped her coat in the chair beside her and looked around the restaurant for a friendly face.

"Cora!" Dorothy waved a menu at her. "Tea?"

"Yes, please." Cora nodded and Dorothy went to get her a pot of hot water. "That is Dorothy Parrish." Walter turned his head when Cora pointed. "Her husband, Frank, stays in the kitchen most of the time, but you might see him at the window from time to time."

Cora held her palm open as Dorothy approached their table with her hot tea and a glass of water. "Dot, this is Walter Slope."

Dorothy nodded. "Nice to meet you."

"Walter is the new manager out at the mine."

"Ah! What a coincidence. I was just asking some

patrons this morning if they knew who was in charge out there now."

"Uh oh," Walter chuckled.

"Dorothy lives out that way," Cora explained. "Not all the way to Miner's Meadow, but on that same road."

"I see," Walter nodded. "I hope the mine doesn't present any problems for you. We try to be respectful of the surrounding community."

"Since when does the mine work on a Sunday?" Dorothy parked a hand on each of her hips after placing the drinks on the table.

"Excuse me?" Walter's forehead wrinkled.

"Sunday!" Dorothy shifted her weight to her other hip. "They were working at the mine. They were blasting."

"No," Walter said, vigorously shaking his head. "That can't be. We weren't working Sunday. I wasn't in town, but I didn't authorize anyone to work."

"Well, they were there. It was just after twelve o'clock noon. Frank and I were coming back from church, and we heard it. He drove down there, and I saw workers on the back fence. There were two guys there, and we heard a total of three blasts. It might have been going on before we returned, but it was shaking the glass in our windows."

"I know blasting is not popular, but it really is necessary sometimes. We have some tunnels to close but it's not going to continue. I wasn't aware of anything planned Sunday, but I'll definitely look into it for you."

"Hey, Dot!" Police Chief Conrad Harris walked up behind Dorothy Parish and lifted his hat. "Am I too late to order?"

"Join us!" Cora Mae picked up her coat from the chair next to her and slung it over the back of her chair.

"Hey, Chief. Never too late to order," Dorothy softened her expression. "Let me get you a place setting."

"I wasn't sure you would get a chance to eat today with the search still going on." Cora Mae slid her place setting toward Conrad as Dorothy placed a new one in front of her.

"Any luck yet?" Dorothy asked Conrad.

"Not much. Briscoe is still out there. There's a lot of territory to cover, and it's not easy walking."

"There's a search?" Walter looked from Cora to Conrad.

"Oh, I'm sorry." Cora shook her head to scold herself. "Chief, this is Walter Slope, the new mine manager. This is our police chief, Conrad Harris."

"A pleasure," Walter said. "I'm new in town and it sounds like there's a lot going on that I'm missing."

"I'd say," Dorothy huffed. "Let me get your orders in before the rush. The specials are on the board." Dorothy pointed to the chalk board near the door.

"I'll take the special," Conrad said.

"For me also." Cora looked at Walter, who shrugged.

"That sounds like the highly regarded choice." Walter chuckled. "I'll give that a try, too."

Dorothy nodded and left the table with a trace of scowl remaining.

"Did I miss something?" Conrad looked at Cora.

"You and me, both." Walter raised his eyebrows.

"Before you walked in, Dorothy was saying that she heard blasting at the mine Sunday." Cora pointed at Walter. “She was asking Walter about that.”

“On a Sunday?” Conrad leaned back in his chair.

“I was out of town, but as far as I know there should not have been anything happening on Sunday.”

“Hmm,” Conrad frowned. “The sheriff's office is out near there now searching for a missing woman. Did you know about that?”

“No, I hadn't heard any local news.” Walter shook his head.

“The woman missing is married to one of your employees.” Conrad raised an eyebrow. “Peter Jessup. Do you know him?”

“I've met him, yes.” Walter looked down at his water glass. “In fact, I spoke with him Friday afternoon.”

“I think you can probably expect to hear from the sheriff's office tomorrow.” Conrad held up his hands to close the conversation. This was not his case and the sheriff's office hadn't shared any information with him about what they planned to do.

“I'm happy to cooperate with anything they need.” Walter sighed and swiveled in his chair to change the subject. “So, tell me Chief, have you always lived in Spicetown? So many people I've met so far seem to have lived here their entire life. I told the mayor, I visited here as a young lad. My grandparents lived here, and I spent some of my summers here.”

“No, I'm a transplant, a late comer, but I'm happy to be here now. Do you think you'll be sticking around? It seems mine managers just don't last long around here.”

“I hope so. If I can accomplish what I came for, I plan to stick around for a long time.” Walter smiled warmly at Cora Mae ignoring Conrad's grimace.

"Here you go," Dot said as she slid the platters of chicken fried steak in front of each of them.

"Thank you, Dot. It's looks delicious."

"Grace Keslar came by this morning," Dorothy said to Cora in a lowered voice. "I guess you know about that party. Frank and I are catering it."

"Yes, I heard about it, but I haven't seen Grace lately."

"Well, she came in here this morning to give me another change to the menu." Dorothy rolled her eyes. "And she offered Jason a job right in front of me! Can you believe that? Here he is working for me, and she offers him a job out at that new fancy spa. As if I don't have enough trouble staffing this place."

"Did Jason take it?" Cora frowned. She had tried to help Dorothy and Frank all summer but finding someone who could cook like Frank was just impossible. Georgia Marks' son, Jason, had been working alongside Frank for the last two years and was doing a great job.

"He did. She says it's just part-time, but I guess I'm supposed to work around that now?"

"I'm sorry, Dot. I hope Jason puts your scheduling needs first." Cora placed her napkin in her lap.

"I'm afraid he's going to work himself to exhaustion. This job isn't light duty by itself and now he's going to run some exercise group at night."

"I'll ask his mom about it," Conrad said with a wink. "Georgia will keep an eye on him."

Dorothy pointed at Conrad and smiled. "Thanks, Chief. Enjoy your meal!"

§

Jill Seabrook took a deep breath. "Mrs. Keslar? I'm so sorry to bother you, but—"

"You are no bother, dear. In fact, I was planning to call you this afternoon anyway." Grace leaned back and tapped her pen on her pad of paper.

"You asked if there was anything else I needed this morning and I hadn't walked around the building yet when I answered. I took some workers to the back of the building after lunch. I wanted to show them the trench back there that needs to be filled in and I saw some damage to our roof."

"The roof is damaged? How could that happen?"

"I don't know. It looks like a big hole was punched in it. It tore right through the shingles and everything. I couldn't believe it. I took some pictures and I'll send them to you, but we will need a roofer pretty quickly. If it rains—"

"Yes, I understand. I think I will get an insurance agent out there first. When was the last time you walked around the back of the building?" Grace opened her desk drawer and began looking for the business card of her insurance agent.

"Last Thursday, I think. I met the truck from the lumberyard when they pulled around back to deliver. I didn't look at the roof, so I couldn't swear it was okay, but I think one of the guys would have noticed even if I hadn't."

"Okay, dear. Let me see what I can do."

"Thank you. Oh, and you said you wanted to talk to me?"

"Yes, about your assistant. I have some concerns." Grace tapped the pad of paper and bit her bottom lip.

"Oh, do you know her?"

"We have not met before, no, but I know of her and I'm not convinced she will be a proper fit for you. I will give it some time, but I wanted you to know my views on the subject."

"Okay," Jill said slowly. "So, what does that mean exactly?"

"I recommend you pay close attention to her actions and don't provide her opportunities to disappoint you. It is always good to test a new hire. Just make certain that her failure will not cause you any loss. Do you understand what I'm saying?"

"Uh, I think so," Jill said. "I'll keep an eye on her."

"As will I. We will talk again soon."

Chapter 9

Conrad mopped the remaining gravy on his plate with his last bite of roll and tossed it in his mouth. Cora and Walter had barely eaten their lunch while they compared childhoods, favorite books, and dream vacation ideas. Conrad wasn't certain why Cora had invited him unless he was meant to save her from a bad blind date. Conrad questioned Walter's intentions and Cora's practical reasoning, but it wasn't his date to judge. When his cell phone vibrated in his shirt pocket as he swallowed his last bite, the timing was magical.

The text from dispatch merely said, *body found.* Conrad tossed his napkin on top of his plate and stood up. "Gotta run." Conrad pointed at Walter. "Nice to meet you." Then pointing at Cora, he said, "I'll talk to you later."

Without waiting for a reply, he slipped his arm in his coat, held his credit card up in the air as Dorothy buzzed by him to snatch it from his hand. "Put it all on there. I'll drop back by later and pick it up."

"Gotcha, Chief." Dorothy knew the routine.

Conrad didn't let anyone buy him lunch and when he had to run out, he always bought the table. He trusted them to hold his card until he returned.

Jumping in his squad car, which was parked on Fennel Street, he headed north to the search area and hit the speed dial for dispatch.

"Hey, Georgie. What do you know?"

"Not much, Chief. Kimball said Briscoe found her. She was a quarter mile from where he found the camera. No blood trail between the two spots."

"That's odd. I guess she could have dropped the camera and run from something." Conrad hummed. "Maybe something else took the camera and carried it."

"Something else? Like an animal?"

"Could be," Conrad said. "It had a strap on it. What kind of condition was she in?"

"Kimball didn't say."

"I'm headed out there now. Briscoe is probably exhausted. Sergeant Cantrell said they may need our interview rooms over the next few days, so give everybody a heads up about that."

"Okay, Chief. See you soon."

Conrad pulled up beside a deputy's cruiser and looked around for an officer he recognized. No ambulance had arrived yet, but he spied Detective Sam Snell talking to two deputies and got out of his car.

"Hey, Sam. Have you seen Kimball?"

"Not yet. I just got here. She's at the scene," Sam pointed into the woods. "In there somewhere."

"Okay." Conrad zipped up his coat. It always seemed colder out here somehow.

"We're waiting on the bus. Officer Pate is going to

take them in. He knows where they are."

"Howdy, Chief. Joshua Pate."

Conrad shook Officer Pate's hand.

"You can follow me in. The bus is pulling up now."

"Great! Appreciate it." Conrad stood to the side waiting for Officer Pate to organize the paramedics and crime scene staff. Once they started through the trees, he quietly followed and marveled at the twists and turns. He was glad he wasn't trying to take this walk alone. Looking up the trees did not seem dense. He saw blue sky and bare branches, but in front of him, there was nothing but bramble blocking his every step. After twenty minutes of walking, he saw Gwen Kimball standing up ahead.

"Hey, Chief." Gwen smiled as Briscoe jumped and jerked the leash against her leg. "He's pretty proud of himself."

Conrad crouched in front of Briscoe to rub his ears and tell him what a good dog he was. Briscoe knew without those words that he had accomplished something significant.

Gwen laughed when Briscoe licked Conrad's face before he could stand up.

"I brought a snack. I'm sure he's tired. You're quite a way from the road here." Conrad pulled some treats from his coat pocket and offered one to Briscoe.

"Yeah, and this is not near the area you found the camera in this morning."

"Nope." Conrad took the leash, and they all stepped back to give the technicians more room. "I don't know why she was so far from her camera."

"This is still close to the mine property," Kimball said pointing through the trees. "It's just not as clear as the place her camera was found. We walked up through there and the back fence to the mine is only about twenty feet that way."

"Sam is here. I think he just got here a little before I did. I don't know if he's been assigned to look into this or he just heard she was found." Conrad motioned for Kimball to follow Officer Pate. "Let's get out of here while we can. This is Joshua Pate, and he knows the way out."

Officer Pate laughed and greeted Officer Kimball. "Follow me."

"Do you know if they developed the film yet?" Gwen scurried to keep up with Officer Pate. "It would be interesting to see what she was taking pictures of back here. It's just a bunch of sticks. I can't wait to get out of here."

Officer Pate looked over his shoulder. "No, I know they've got the film, but I haven't heard about any result yet."

Conrad followed behind the group with Briscoe at a leisurely pace. Briscoe was the only one who truly knew the way out and Conrad had learned to trust him. After the long walk and they parted through the final thicket of twigs and branches, the officers waiting by their cars began applauding when they saw Briscoe walk through the clearing.

Sensing he was getting his fifteen minutes of fame, Briscoe barked and jumped in response to the clapping until Conrad squatted down beside him to assure him that the attention was indeed his reward.

§

"Now what's going on down there?" David Dorn tossed the supplies in the back of Noah's pickup truck and stopped to listen to the voices. "Do you hear that?"

"Yeah. I don't know. Something must be going on down by the road."

"They're making a lot of noise." David frowned. They were on the backside of the Paxton Mine property and there shouldn't be anyone nearby for miles.

"We need to get over to the other side and unload this. I've got a meeting at four o'clock in Paxton. I can't be hanging out here all afternoon." Noah Yates climbed into the cab of his truck and waited for David to get in the passenger seat.

"Did you get your letter from the State yet?" Noah had to turn the key and pump the gas pedal several times to get the old truck to start.

"No, but I don't have the thirty hours of class time done yet, so I know I'm not going to get my certification."

"You've done the two years as a blaster apprentice though, right? Didn't you tell me you worked with Scott Murphy for over a year?"

"Yeah."

"Well, I mailed in a certificate for you saying you've been with me for a year, so that takes care of your time requirement for a blaster's certificate." Noah shrugged. David had only been with him for about four months, but he seemed to know what he was doing. All of those State requirements were a waste of time. Either you were good at blowing up rock or you weren't.

"I'm not sure my time with you is going to count. If they look up and see you're suspended by West Virginia, they might not count my time working with you. I don't know how that works."

"Nonsense. They won't even check. They don't care."

"I'll be done with the classes in April."

"That will be good. You can get your blaster certification then and that will double your salary." Noah nodded. He hoped to be independently wealthy by then. "You can have my job."

"Uh, I don't know about that." David shook his head. "I have to pass an exam and I'm horrible at tests."

"Son! What did you get into this business for if you don't think you can cut it? You can't be an apprentice your whole life."

"I thought it sounded easy and I wouldn't have to work with other people. I don't like crowds and I don't like going in the mines. My dad suggested it. He thought I could do it."

"I know you can. There's nothing to it." Noah pulled his truck up next to a storage building. "Let's unload the stuff here and then I'll run to Paxton."

"Okay. Are we working this site tomorrow?" David pulled the tailgate down.

"I'm not sure yet. We'll have to wait and see what the boss says. He should be back tomorrow. It may be a few days before we can continue with the tunnels."

"Okay, I guess, but I can't sit around idle like this. I need the work."

"Are you looking for a way to make a little extra cash?" Noah grinned mischievously.

"I don't know. What do you have in mind?" David drew back with a leery expression.

"Uh, I may have a little side job tonight. I can cut

you in, if you need the money. Just asking."

"If it's not illegal, I'd be interested. I can always use the cash."

"Well, hey. You can't be picky now." Noah laughed as he tossed the boxes into the storage building. "I'll let you know after my meeting."

"Okay," David said as he slammed the tailgate shut.

Chapter 10

Conrad stood up and stretched. He was ready to end this long day but returned to his seat when he heard footsteps heading toward his office.

"Are you still here, Chief?" Gwen Kimball peeked around the doorway and smiled.

"Still here, but I'm about ready to leave."

"Sam is here." Gwen stepped back as Detective Sam Snell walked through the door.

"The Sheriff assigned me to the Jessup case." Sam tugged on his belt. "He told me to ask you if we could use your interview rooms. He wants me to talk to all of the miners."

"Cantrell already asked and there's no problem. You're welcome to any space I have that's not in use." Conrad waved his hand toward the chair across from his desk. "Have a seat. Do you have any information to work with yet?"

"Blunt force trauma to the head." Sam shrugged. "Autopsy is tomorrow, but apparently the wound speaks for itself."

"Yes, but did you get a look at it? It doesn't look like it's from a fall to me." Conrad glanced at Gwen standing in the doorway and Gwen nodded her head in agreement.

"No?" Sam frowned. "I thought it was the back of her head."

"It was the top of her head." Conrad placed his hand on the top of his head and patted it. "I don't see how a fall could have caused that."

"Oh!" Sam's shoulders reared back. "I didn't realize that. I didn't get to examine her. They loaded her up too quickly."

"Did the techs find anything around the body?"

"I don't have that report yet." Sam looked over his shoulder at Gwen. "Did you see anything?"

"No, nothing and Briscoe didn't react to the area around her either." Gwen held her hands out. "I hope the autopsy shows something to give you a clue about what happened."

"I still think it was an accident." Sam stood up and brushed his hand over the leg of his jeans. "Maybe there's something more to it, but it seems pretty innocent. It was really bad out there. I don't know why anyone would want to walk in that mess, but I guess pictures were important to her."

"Maybe when you get the film developed, you'll find out whether it was worth the walk." Conrad chuckled.

"Maybe, but the other guys sure think the husband had something to do with it. I haven't met him yet. I guess he was there before I showed up and they talked to him, but then he went home. It sounds like they were estranged."

"You would think he could at least stick around

and pretend to care," Gwen said.

"I think the relationship may be more complicated than that," Conrad said as he shifted in his chair. "I could be wrong, but I think she was reported missing by another miner, a guy named Trevor Mason, who claims to be a friend. He was the one supplying a personal item for Briscoe to get a scent. I think he may be closer to the victim than her husband."

"Ah, an open marriage perhaps?" Sam grinned.

"Maybe, but the husband is a miner, too, which means the guys must know each other. They work together."

"This could be messy!" Sam laughed. "You have motivated me to dive in! I'll be in early tomorrow and get started with my interviews. This could actually turn out to be an interesting case."

§

"Mom, I'm sorry. I should have called. There was just a lot going on."

"Let me heat up some dinner for you. Sit down right there." Marissa Jessup pointed, and Peter sat.

"It's crazy down there. The police think Jane went into the woods this morning and never came out. They're climbing all over the place out there."

"Well, did she? Are you sure that crazy girl didn't just walk out?" Marissa put a plate into the microwave.

"I don't think so. I mean she didn't say anything to me about leaving. Why would she?"

"Did you check to see if she took anything? She might have emptied all your bank accounts. Is her jewelry there?"

"Uh, I don't know. I've only been home a minute, and the police were with me. I didn't notice anything that looked different."

"That's the first thing you need to check. You will stay the night here tonight and we'll go over there tomorrow and check things out. This all sounds completely irrational, but that's Jane for you. The girl is crazy as the day is long. I swear I'll never understand what you saw in her."

"She's not crazy, Mom. We just had some problems."

"I don't want to hear about it." Marissa tossed her hands in the air and then jumped when the microwave timer went off. Sliding the plate in front of Peter, she turned to open the refrigerator. "Do you want tea to drink, dear?"

"Yeah."

Marissa pulled out a chair at the kitchen table across from Peter and took a sip of tea. "Be honest with me, honey. What kind of situation are you and Jane living in now? She hasn't been taking my calls at all. I leave her messages and she doesn't answer me."

"You know you guys have never gotten along, Mom. That's nothing new."

"But she used to at least respond to me! I was afraid she was leaving you, trying to file for divorce! She has nothing, no way to support herself and she would try to take everything you've worked so hard for. I can't just sit by and let her ruin your life."

"What did you do, Mom? Did you say something to her?"

"I can't get you to do anything about it. Yes, I've left her messages, but she won't talk to me."

"What did you say?"

Marissa waved his question away. “Are you trying to work things out?”

“No, not really. We don’t talk much anymore, but we aren’t fighting. Please just stay out of it, Mom.”

Marissa turned in her chair when she heard a knock at the front door. “Who could that be?” Walking toward the door, she saw the uniforms through the window. “It’s the police.”

Peter wiped his hands on a napkin and got up from the table to follow.

“Good evening, Mrs. Jessup. I’m Sergeant Cantrell with the sheriff’s office and we’re looking for your son, Peter.” A uniformed deputy stood behind the Sergeant and nodded hello.

“That’s me, Officer.” Peter walked in front of his mother and opened the screen door.

“May we come inside?”

“Sure.” Peter pushed the screen door open and sat down on the couch.

“We were just having dinner. Can we get you anything?” Marissa fluttered around the kitchen door nervously. “Something to drink at least?”

“No, ma’am. Thank you.”

Peter motioned to the officers to sit and leaned forward with his elbows on his thighs. “Can I help with something? Are you still looking?”

“No, sir. We wanted to tell you that we did find your wife, Jane. I’m so—”

“Oh! That’s great! Where was she? So, everything’s okay now?”

“No, sir. I’m sorry to have to tell you this, but we found your wife’s body in the woods.”

“She’s dead!” Peter started to stand up and then sat back down. “Jane’s dead. How did she die? What happened?"

"She's with the coroner now and there will be an autopsy. We hope that will help address some of those questions, but for right now all I can tell you is that she had a head injury."

Marissa dropped to the couch next to Peter and put her arm around his shoulders. "Oh, my goodness, son. I'm so sorry. This is terrible. Poor Jane. That dear girl. How could this happen?"

"We apologize for the late hour, but we had some difficulty locating you. You haven't been answering your cell phone, and you weren't at home."

"My cell?" Peter pulled it from his back pocket. "Oh, I think I turned the ringer off." Olivia had called repeatedly wanting status updates, and he had grown tired of the questions. "I'm sorry. I forgot about it."

"We need to take a statement from you, and we'd like you to come down to the Spicetown Police Department to—"

"Oh, can't that wait until tomorrow, Sergeant?" Marissa hugged her son. "It's late and we are still in a state of shock here."

"Certainly." Sergeant Cantrell stood up and walked to the door with the deputy following. "I will let Detective Snell know to expect you at eight o'clock tomorrow morning at the Spicetown Police Department." The sergeant stared directly at Peter until he looked away.

"Yeah. Yes, I'll be there."

"Thank you, and we're very sorry for your loss."

"Thank you, Sergeant."

Marissa jogged to the door and locked it before returning to the kitchen. "Come finish your dinner, honey. Do you want me to heat it back up? It's probably cold now."

"No, mom. I've got to think." Peter held his hands open in front of him. "I've got to think about this. They're going to try to trick me tomorrow. They're going to ask a lot of questions to make me look guilty. I didn't have anything to do with this, Mom."

"Of course, you didn't, dear."

"They're going to want to know where I was."

"Yes. You just tell them where you were, and they won't bother you anymore. Do you have witnesses? Where were you Sunday morning?"

Peter glanced at his mother and scowled. "I'd rather not say. That's the problem. It doesn't have anything to do with Jane, but I don't want to tell them. They'll make something out of it and it's nothing."

"What's nothing, dear? Where were you?"

"At a friend's house."

"Is it a friend that I know?" Marissa slowly sat down in the chair across from Peter.

"No, you don't know her."

"It was a female friend?"

"Yeah, but—"

"Peter, are you having an affair with this friend?" Marissa stood up and put her hands on her hips. "You need to answer me right now, because if you are, we need to have a plan in place. You're right. They're going to try to lock you up for this. We need to get you a lawyer and you better talk to this girl before the police do."

"Let me think!" Peter shouted. "I need to think."

"You need to do more than that, young man. You need to call this girl right now. Did she know Jane was missing? She has motive, you know. Are you sure she didn't do something to Jane?"

"I'm sure. She doesn't even know Jane. She's not from Spicetown. She's never even seen Jane before and she definitely didn't have anything to do with all this."

"How do you know that?" Marissa waved her arms in the air. "How do you know she didn't lure her out of the house this morning and kill her in the woods? You don't know that."

"Actually, yes I do," Peter said calmly. Leaning back against the couch he looked up at his mom. "I was with her all evening and all morning. In fact, I was at her house when the police called me to say Jane was missing, so I know she didn't have anything to do with it."

"Okay," Marissa frowned. "Well, there's your alibi. You better not make her mad at you. Get her over here. We need to get all of our ducks in a row."

Chapter 11

Cora grabbed her phone when she saw Conrad was calling. "Hi, Connie. I was just thinking about you. Any update on the girl?"

"Yeah, Briscoe found her, but she's been dead for a while."

"Oh, mercy," Cora groaned. "That's awful. It is especially hard around the holiday season. Is her family here?"

"I don't know all those details. Detective Snell is going to do some interviewing tomorrow at the station, so maybe he'll figure something out. Sorry to call so late, but I didn't want you to hear it on the news first."

"Oh, no. I'm glad you called. I was worried about her. Walter was telling me that he had some words with her husband Friday at work. Some disagreement about a safety protocol apparently. He said he's having trouble with him. I believe the young man's name is Peter."

"That's him."

"Amanda said he is a friend of Bryan's. I think

they were in the same class in school together. I don't know the boy myself, but—"

"You don't know him?" Conrad didn't hear that from Cora very often.

"No, he wasn't a student of mine. I had his older brother and I do know his mother. She's a domineering force. I suspect the young man is rather meek from growing up in that environment."

"Is Walter liking his new job okay? He didn't mention much about it at lunch."

"He hasn't said specifically. We talked again tonight, and that's when he mentioned his disagreement with Peter. Other than that, we haven't talked about his work."

"Hmm, Walter's not been at work much. From what I hear, he was all over town today."

"He did tell me he's visited several businesses. He's trying to get to know the area."

"Yes, I was just surprised he wasn't needed at the mine. I've never known the other managers to gallivant around town so much."

"He's not gallivanting! And he actually lives here. The others took lodging in Paxton instead."

"Okay, I just thought it odd. He certainly does make an effort to win friends and influence people."

"You say that like it's a bad thing," Cora gasped. "I'm beginning to think you don't like Walter Slope."

"I can't say I'm informed enough to vote on that subject just yet." Conrad chuckled. "I'll try to reserve judgment."

"Would you like to have dinner tomorrow night? I'm going to pop in for a few minutes of play practice at the community center, then I can meet you at the Old Thyme Italian at six o'clock. Maybe Sam and

Gwen would like to join us."

"I'll ask them if he's free. I don't know what tomorrow is going to be like for him. Have you been keeping up with play practice? I never heard of this play they're doing."

"It's new to me too, and no, I haven't watched any of the practice yet. Saucy has me curious though. He won't tell me what he's doing, but he says it's a surprise."

"Then maybe you need to wait until opening night and let him surprise you!" Conrad laughed. "You can't stand it though, can you?"

"You know me so well." Cora Mae chuckled. "I wish he'd never said anything because now I can't stand not knowing. I tried to get Walter to tell me tonight, and he said Saucy swore him to secrecy. It's going to drive me batty."

"It sounds like cheating to me. I don't think you should go to practice. You should just let Saucy have his big moment."

"I know, but I'd like to see Walter, too. I bet he's a really wonderful actor."

"That I can agree with you on." Conrad gritted his teeth. "I'll see you tomorrow at six."

§

"Now you call me back!?" Walter Slope shouted into his cell phone. "Where have you been?"

"What do you mean? I'm here. Where am I supposed to be?" Noah Yates chuckled. "Settle down old man. What do you need?"

Walter clenched his teeth. "I need for you to show up to work. You were hired to do a job. If you want to get paid, you have to be present."

"I was there!"

"No, you weren't. I looked for you all afternoon and nobody had seen you."

"I moved the stuff out to the storage building on the west side. Me and David did. That's all you told me to do."

"And then what? Where did you go?"

"What? You want me to sit around an office all day like you do? If you don't have any work for me, I didn't figure I needed to hang around."

"Well, you're wrong." Walter sat down and lowered his forehead into the palm of his hand. "You're new. You've got to expect the others are watching you. I've already got the union inquiring. The others are working full shifts. You can't just flit around doing whatever you want to do all day. You've got to be present, be seen, and do something. David, too."

"Yeah, okay."

"And most of all, you have to respond to me. I can explain away your absence on occasion, but when I call, you *call back*! Do you understand me?"

"Yeah. Yeah, I got it. Cool your jets. So, what's on the agenda tomorrow?"

"I got nothing."

Noah laughed. "You got nothing for me to do and you complain I'm not around to do it!"

"I'm getting complaints already." Walter yelled. "I need to let it rest for a day or two."

"That always happens."

"Not usually the very first time. You guys got too close and why did you do it on a Sunday? What were you thinking?"

"What difference does that make? I thought it was a good time. Everybody was gone and out of the way."

"You're an idiot," Walter hissed. "There are laws about that stuff. Blasting has to be approved by corporate and the community has to receive notice. I put the schedule in the paper, for heaven's sake! You can't just do it when you think it feels right! Did you just fall off the back of a truck on your head?"

"Hey!"

Walter took a deep breath and blew it out slowly in an attempt to calm his nerves. The boy was so frustrating. "Look, I don't mean to yell. I'm a little frustrated right now. I'm getting a lot of pressure from all sides. The union wants to bargain every change I make, corporate wants to question or approve every thought I have, the townspeople are complaining about the blasting, and I still have nineteen months to retirement. I'm just trying to get there in one piece."

"I get it. Don't worry about it. It'll all be fine."

"That's easy for you to say."

Noah laughed. "Yeah, I guess it is."

"Do you know about the missing girl?" Walter popped a fresh toothpick in his mouth. "The police are looking for some girl that got lost walking back behind the property. You and David need to keep an eye out if you go in that area."

"Is that what the helicopter was about?" Noah gasped. "That happened Sunday night and it kind of freaked me out for a minute."

"You need to stay away from that area completely for now. It's swarming with cops."

"No problem. We're going to hit the west side next, on the other side of the ridge. There's nothing much out there."

Walter huffed. "There's a church out there, so make sure you don't do anything on the weekend."

"Gotcha, boss." Noah chuckled.

"There's another business across from the church, too. I saw it last week when I drove out there." Walter frowned. "There were cars in the parking lot, but I don't know what it is."

"Yeah, it's some new business that isn't open yet. They were probably just working on the building. Don't worry about it. I've got it all handled."

Walter bit down on the toothpick but it didn't offer any relief. "Okay," Walter said, shaking his head. "Tell your mother I said hello when you talk to her."

"Ha! I'll talk to you tomorrow."

Chapter 12

"Morning, Chief." Officer Eugene Tabor met Conrad in the hallway as soon as he entered through the side door. Guiding Briscoe into his office, he released the leash from his harness and Briscoe curled up in his dog bed near the credenza.

"Morning, Tabor. We're probably going to have a busy day around here today. The sheriff's office is going to do some interviewing in here—"

"Oh, they're already here, Chief. The front lobby is full of people. It sounds like everybody was told to be here at eight o'clock. I guess they thought the interviews would be quick." Tabor shrugged. "I don't know, but there's a little bit of chaos."

"Is Sam Snell here?"

"No, not yet. Georgia called him though and let him know about everybody waiting on him. He's on his way. Are we supposed to help interview?"

"I didn't think so, but it sounds like Sam may need some help. I'll ask him when he gets here."

"The husband is here." Tabor cleared his throat.

"The victim's husband, Peter Jessup. I put him in Interview Room 4 because there was some tension out there. I get the impression the other guys don't like him much. It's kind of a rough group out there."

"Really? You'd think they would be sympathetic. I mean the guy just lost his wife!"

"I know, Chief, but it doesn't seem that they are."

Conrad picked up his pitcher and headed to the break room for water, but Tabor followed.

"Chief, before you do that, Grace Keslar called and asked for us to come out to her house this morning. She wants to file a report."

Conrad frowned. "What kind of report?"

"She said she needs to report vandalism and theft." Tabor widened his eyes innocently. "I told her she should call the Sheriff's Office. She doesn't live in Spicetown city limits, but she said it was for her new business, not her home."

"The spa? It's not in Spicetown either!"

Tabor laughed. "I mentioned that, but she didn't feel like that should matter. I'm guessing she wants to file the report just as a formality because she's making an insurance claim. I offered to take the details over the phone for her, but she insisted that she wants me and you to come out there."

Conrad sighed. "Let me call her. Maybe I can talk her down."

"Morning, Chief." Sam Snell walked into the break room with an empty coffee cup. "Is it okay if I get some coffee?"

"Sure." Conrad pointed to the coffee pot on the counter that the staff used. Conrad had his own in his office that he rarely shared. "You've got quite an audience out there today. Do you need help with interviews?"

"I was supposed to have two officers assigned here this morning, but they got pulled. Something bigger going on somewhere else I suppose. It happens all the time." Detective Snell filled his coffee cup. "I'd appreciate any help you can offer. Most of them are just miners we couldn't reach over the weekend. We need to know whether they saw the victim walking and gather whatever info we can about the husband and boyfriend."

"So, we are officially calling Trevor Mason a boyfriend now?" Conrad snickered.

"Unofficially." Sam smiled. "I haven't talked to him yet, but the other guys at the scene felt like it was an appropriate title."

"It seemed that way to me, too." Conrad nodded. "He definitely knows a lot more about the victim than one would expect."

"The victim's husband is in Interview Room 4, Detective Snell."

"Thank you."

Eugene Tabor walked out of the break room and Conrad filled his pitcher with water. "That's Tabor." Conrad pointed at the door. "He said he got the impression the other guys out there don't get along with the husband. That's why he put him in a room. I didn't know there were bad vibes out at the mine, but I thought you should know before you talk to him. Maybe he can tell you why."

"Thanks, Chief."

"I've gotta make a call this morning and then I'll see if I can get you some help."

"Appreciate it."

Conrad returned to his coffee maker and set up his

chicory and cinnamon mixture so it would be ready once the water heated. Then he reached for his desk phone. Smiling at Briscoe curled up in his bed, he had the perfect plan for Mrs. Keslar.

"Good morning. This is Chief Conrad Harris of the Spicetown Police Department. I'm returning a call to Mrs. Grace Keslar. Is she available?"

"Yes, sir, Chief. Let me get her for you." The response was a male voice, so Conrad assumed it was Stanley, her driver. He had been with her when she had stopped by the station to invite everyone to her Christmas party. Conrad was glad to see the happy, friendly Grace he met over a decade ago had finally returned. She had been the life of the party until her husband, Chancellor, died. Then she had gone into hiding so long that he had given up on ever seeing her again.

"Good morning, Conrad," Grace chirped. "It's lovely to hear from you. It's a beautiful day outside, albeit a bit chilly. Have you been outside today?"

"Yes, ma'am. I have. I got a message that you needed to see me, but I'm just not going to be able to come out there today. I'm going to have my dog with me and so I was calling to see if we could get your information down by telephone. I know your cat doesn't like to have dogs around." Conrad winked at Briscoe.

"Oh, no, Chief. I'm sorry, but I can't explain it over the phone. I need for you to see it, not at my house, but out at the spa."

"Well, I'm helping the Sheriff today with a case. Did you hear about the poor girl in the woods? They found her body yesterday and there are a lot of people to interview. It's going to keep me tied up here all day. Could I send an officer to your spa?"

Grace sighed.

"He can take pictures for me and then I'll be able to see it." Conrad paused, but Grace didn't concede, so he moved to Plan B. "Or I could come out tomorrow morning."

"Oh well, I guess London can handle it. If it has to be..."

"I don't want you to have to wait too long." Conrad pushed the button on his coffee maker.

"I guess it will be okay if you can send London. I talked to him this morning. Is he still there?"

"Yes, ma'am. I can send London. When do you want to meet him?" Conrad leaned back in his chair to stifle his laughter.

"I can go out there right now. Can he do that? I'll jump in the car right now and be there when he gets there."

"I'll tell him. Have a good day, Mrs. Keslar."

"You, too, Chief. And good luck on your hunt."

Conrad chuckled as he hung up the phone and walked into the hallway.

"London!" Conrad hollered down the hallway toward the dispatch cubicle and saw Georgia Marks giggle. "London, I need to send you out."

"Chief?" Tabor hung his head in embarrassment. Grace had officially dubbed him London when she first met him because she thought he should guard the Big Ben and wear a tall hat. He did have a very statuesque posture and Conrad had agreed with her. "You talked to her?"

"I did. I got myself out of it but couldn't do much for you. She's on her way out to the spa right now and you need to meet her. Take a bunch of pictures for me."

Conrad laughed as he walked back to his office but stopped when he realized Georgia was on his heels holding out phone message slips. Conrad moaned and took them from her hand.

"Sheriff Bell called and said he wants to talk to you."

"I cannot do that without coffee."

"Also, Hazel Linton called to say she's hearing gunfire around the lake. She doesn't need a call back. She just wanted you to know that 'some dang fool is shootin' up the place'. Her words, not mine."

Conrad smiled and nodded. "Thank you, Georgie. Oh, Georgia! I heard your son is going to work out at the new spa."

Georgia's jaw clenched. "He's talking about it. I haven't encouraged him."

"I know Dorothy is worried he's going to exhaust himself. She was a little upset that Mrs. Keslar came into the restaurant and offered him the job right in front of her. Dorothy really depends on Jason."

"I know." Georgia nodded. "I have reservations about it, too, for different reasons, but I've voiced them to him. He's a grown man so I've got to give him a chance to make the right decision."

"If he decides to take it, I'm curious about what name he's going to get. Aren't you?" Conrad smiled timidly.

"If he takes it, she won't need to give him a name. I've already got one all picked out for him." Georgia looked over the top of her glasses at Conrad and turned on her heel.

Conrad hoped the boy made the right choice for everybody's sake.

§

"There's a cop outside," Olivia whispered to Jill and then scurried around the desk to the front doors.

"Hello?" Eugene rapped on the glass door with his flashlight. "I'm Officer Tabor and I'm supposed to be meeting Mrs. Keslar out here this morning."

"Are you going to just stand there and stare at the man?" Jill barked. "Open the door!"

"Sorry," Olivia said as she flipped the lock and pulled the door open. "Sorry, but Mrs. Keslar isn't here yet, but you can come inside."

"Thank you." Tabor removed his hat and nodded to Jill. "She asked me to meet her this morning to file a report. She mentioned a theft and some damage she wanted photographed."

Jill pushed Olivia out of the way. "Yes, we had some roof damage but I'm not sure why she called you."

"Was it vandalism?"

"Well, I guess it could have been." Jill scowled. "You know I don't really know what it was. It's weird. I can show you if you like. It's around back."

"Mrs. Keslar's here." Olivia pointed through the glass in the front door.

"I'll wait for her," Tabor said. "Thanks."

"We had an earlier theft. Did she report that?"

"She did." Tabor nodded.

"It's weird. You think you're out here in the middle of nowhere and nobody's around, but every time we leave something outside, it gets lifted." Jill slapped her hands against her legs. "It's like somebody is watching us."

"Do you ever see any activity across the street at the church?" Tabor glanced out the door to see if the church was visible.

"You think the church people are robbing us?!" Olivia laughed nervously.

"No, ma'am. I thought maybe they might have seen visitors here after hours. Their services would be nights and weekends which is the times that you are most likely away from the business."

"That's true." Jill nodded. "I should talk to them. Maybe we can keep an eye on each other's place."

'Maybe so." Tabor smiled.

"London!" Grace came through the door with her hands in the air as if she was going to grab Tabor's face but settled for both of his arms. "Thank you for coming. The Chief told me how busy you all were, and I do appreciate that you could find some time for me."

"Of course, Mrs. Keslar. We were just about to step outside and take a look at the roof."

"Oh! Yes, let's start there. Come along."

Chapter 13

"Long day?" Cora Mae scooted into the booth at the Old Thyme Italian Restaurant. Conrad had already arrived and was reading the menu.

Looking over the top of his glasses, Conrad moaned. "Very busy, but it was interesting."

"Gwen and Sam didn't want to join us?" Cora had hoped to hear details of the case.

"No, they are both out interviewing the ones that didn't show up today. Your friend, Walter, is one of them."

"I saw him at the community center earlier. He didn't mention an interview."

"He was supposed to come down to the station today, but he didn't show."

"Oh, I'm sure there was just a misunderstanding. He must not have been aware that his presence was required, or he would have mentioned it to me." Cora pulled her phone from her purse. "I can text him if you like. I'm sure he'll be happy to come down now or in the morning."

"No need. Sam will handle it. I think he's planning on going out to the mine in the morning to pull any he's still missing off their shift. Maybe Walter will be at work tomorrow."

"I'm sure he will," Cora said, sliding her phone back into her purse. "He doesn't know anything about Jane Jessup, but I know he wouldn't intentionally avoid Sam for any reason."

"Hmm," Conrad mumbled. "So, did you learn Saucy's secret?"

Cora Mae chuckled. "No, I did not. The little rascal has sworn everyone to secrecy, and they didn't practice that part of the play tonight."

"It opens in two days, doesn't it?"

"It does! I have tickets for the Sunday matinée, but Thursday night is the first showing."

"What's the play about?" Conrad slipped his glasses back in his pocket.

"It's set in a small town in the 1930's and there are two different groups planning to use the town hall for a Christmas celebration. They both show up at the same time and they have to work through the chaos. That's all I really know. It's a comedy and what little I saw in practice today was really cute. I think it will be fun."

"I just thought it would be more traditional since it's Christmas."

"There is a lot of Christmas music in the play. The school choir is singing also."

"No carolers in the lobby this year?"

"You know, I'm not sure. Shelby handled all of that last year because she was promoting the animal shelter. I need to ask and see if we're doing that again."

"Good evening. Sorry for the delay. Can I take your order?" The young man smiled nervously at Cora Mae.

"I'd like the Stromboli and just some hot water for tea to drink." Cora Mae turned her coffee cup over on the table.

"Okay, and for you, Chief?"

"I'd like the lasagna tonight. Water to drink is fine."

"Great. I'll get your orders right in."

"Thank you, Kevin." Cora Mae smiled when the young man blushed and bowed his head.

"One of your students?" Conrad smirked.

"Once upon a time, yes. He was a shy one, but a very nice boy. Kevin Thurman."

"Is he kin to Nick Thurman? He's one of the miners that Sam is looking for."

"Yes, that's his older brother. There's a sister in between them named Lindsey."

"Gwen interviewed her today."

"Lindsey? Why? She isn't a miner."

"No, but she was dating one. Trevor Mason. Do you know him?"

"Yes." Cora Mae opened her napkin and placed it on her lap.

"No commentary on Trevor Mason?" Conrad was confused by Cora's delayed response. "Just, yes?"

"I heard Trevor was dating Lindsey, but I don't think they are currently seeing one another."

"Really? Could it be that his marriage got in the way?" Conrad continued watching for a reaction. "What do you know?"

"I don't know anything." Cora shook her head. "People talk, of course, but I don't know anything firsthand."

Conrad smirked. "Okay, you don't like to deal in rumors. I get that, but what is the talk you hear?"

Cora Mae frowned and looked around before responding. "The word on the street is that he and his wife are separated, and he is seeing a married woman."

Conrad swallowed his mirth and leaned forward to lower his voice. "That's the word on the street, huh?"

"It is." Cora Mae sat up straight and ignored Conrad's smugness. "I think Trevor is a nice boy and I hope it isn't true, but I am pretty certain that he has broken up with Lindsey because I used to see them at church together."

"Oh, so you saw Trevor on Sunday? That's what Sam is trying to find out."

"I did. He was in the morning service, but he wasn't sitting with Lindsey."

Conrad nodded. He would need to remember to share that with Sam Snell. "Oh, the Sheriff called me today."

Cora looked alarmed. "Whatever for? How did that go?"

"It was strange. First, he wanted to ask me what I thought about Detective Snell dating Officer Kimball. He thought maybe it was a bad idea to let them be involved in the same case. He thought they should be kept apart at work."

"Haven't you already had that conversation with him back when it first began?"

"Yeah, and I explained to him again that I have limited personnel and I don't have the luxury of reassigning officers just because he had staff using my interview rooms. We aren't working this case. We're just accommodating his needs."

"Yikes! How did he take that?"

Conrad chuckled. "Surprisingly well. He said he understood, and he trusted my judgment."

"What?"

Conrad laughed. "I almost said the very same thing to him. Had to pick my jaw up off the desk."

"You're right. That's strange."

Kevin placed their drinks on the table and Cora thanked him.

"Then he asked a bunch of questions about the case that his own officers could have answered. He can read their reports. I have to assume he wanted to know how much I knew."

"Did you play dumb?" Cora grinned.

"Yep."

Cora Mae laughed as Kevin walked up with their order. "Good call."

§

"Have a seat, Peter. Dinner is almost ready." Marissa Jessup placed the salt and pepper shakers on the kitchen table. "I'm dishing it all up now."

"Ma, I'm not hungry. I just stopped by to let you know everything is okay. I'm going home tonight."

"Not so fast. Take a seat and tell me what happened today."

Peter pulled a chair out at the kitchen table and slipped off his coat. "Nothing much. They asked a lot of questions about Jane and stuff. It just seemed like the same thing over and over."

Marissa put a glass of tea next to the place setting in front of Peter. "This girl that's your alibi, have they talked to her yet?"

"Not that I know of. I'll give her a call tonight."

Marissa speared a chicken breast with a fork and placed it on Peter's plate. "Have the two of you talked about this? Do you know what she's going to say?"

Peter placed a napkin across his lap and reached for a dinner roll. "Yeah, she's going to tell them I was with her all morning."

Marissa sat a tub of butter in front of Peter before filling her own plate. "Well, were you?"

"Yeah. Yeah, I was there. I mean I ran out for a minute to grab something to eat but that's where I was when the police called."

"You spent the night there?" Marissa raised a disapproving eyebrow but drilled her gaze into Peter's forehead as he avoided her stare.

"Yeah, but I get up early. I let her sleep."

"They are going to poke a million holes into that. Did you tell the police that? If you did, they're going to think you went out in the woods and killed her."

Peter scowled. "Ah, Ma. That's crazy. It sounds to me like she just fell and hit her head. They aren't trying to pin anything on me."

"You are so naive, my child. Of course, they are. That's what police do. They want to solve crimes and make headlines, so they can impress everyone."

"I think they're just trying to find out what happened."

"Pfft," Marissa waved her hand dismissively. "Think what you want, but this little girl you've got on the side has the power to make a lot of trouble for you. You need to get your story straight. Why don't you invite her over here? I'd like to meet her. Then we can all talk about it together."

"No." Peter shook his head and continued to chew.

"You need to be in control of this situation, Peter."

"Ma, it's not a big deal. Nobody thinks Jane was murdered. It was just an accident, and you don't need to meet Olivia. It's not a serious thing."

"Does she know that?" Marissa widened her eyes and leaned forward. "You've never been able to read women, Peter. That's why you have so much trouble with them."

"What trouble?" Peter pointed at his mother with his fork. "I'm not having any trouble."

"What do you call your entire marriage? It was a disaster." Marissa reached for a napkin. "All you ever did was fight or not speak to one another. She was mad all the time, and you were sulking. You were both miserable."

"That's not true. It just seemed that way to you because you hated her. And a lot of the times our fights were about you or about coming over to your house because she was miserable around you."

"That's just silly. I was always pleasant to her. I did my very best to put up with her because I had to. You put me in that position. You can't blame this on me."

Peter rolled his eyes. "It doesn't matter anymore."

"No, I guess not. What are your plans going forward?" Marissa took a deep breath and sat back in her chair.

"No plans. What do you mean? Nothing's changed."

"Are you going to keep the house?"

"Sure! I gotta have someplace to live." Peter huffed.

"Well, there's no reason for you to pay all that

money on a mortgage when you can move in here with me. I've got lots of room. It's close to your work and you can come or go as you need to. I won't bother you."

"What? No! No, mom. I'm not doing that. I like where I'm at just fine and I need my own space."

"Well, if you change your mind, you're always welcome. Do you want dessert?"

Chapter 14

Detective Sam Snell rapped his knuckles on the door frame to Conrad's open office door. "Good morning, Chief."

"Good morning, detective. Did you find some coffee?"

"Yes, I've been here a couple of hours. I wondered if you had a minute to chat. I can come back later if you're busy this morning."

"Come on in." Conrad motioned him to a chair. "I got in earlier but just got back in from grabbing some breakfast. I had a couple of things I wanted to run by you, too. What's your day looking like today?"

"I'm going out to the mine this morning again. I haven't talked to Walter Slope yet and I have a short list of miners I still want to check with. I haven't found anyone that saw Jane Jessup walking down to the area where she was found."

"That road doesn't get a lot of traffic on a Saturday morning. Other than Miner's Meadow, there's just a slew of farms out that way. Are you thinking she might have gotten there another way?"

"Her car is at her house, so I know she didn't drive. She could have walked it, but it's pretty cold outside."

"Have you interviewed Trevor Mason yet?"

"I have. He said he's just friends with the victim. I interviewed Mason's girlfriend, too. She said he was unaccounted for during part of Sunday morning, so I've got some filling in to do there."

"But do you even have a sign of foul play? I'm not trying to close your case here, but do you have reason to pursue? Did the film get developed? Do you have autopsy results? From standing back in my shoes, it looks like an unfortunate accident."

"That's what I wanted to talk to you about." Sam uncrossed his ankles and leaned forward. "Mind if I shut your door?"

Conrad shook his head. "Before I forget, the mayor told me that Trevor Mason isn't dating Lindsey Thurman anymore. She saw Trevor at church Sunday morning in the service if that's of any help to you. She knows them both. She's also pretty chummy with Walter Slope if you're needing any insight to him."

Sam nodded. "Good to know. Thank you. But what I wanted to discuss with you, I mean I don't have anything solid, but I need somewhere to lay it out. Gwen, Officer Kimball, suggested I talk to you. She said I can trust you."

"She's right. I'm happy to help any way I can. What's on your mind?"

"This would have to stay between us." Sam flipped his index finger like a metronome between himself and Conrad, looking over his shoulder at the closed door.

"Even a fool who keeps silent is considered wise."

Conrad nodded. "I learned that a long time ago."

"Okay." Sam took a deep breath. "It's about Sheriff Bell." Sam studied Conrad for a reaction, but Conrad kept his expression unchanged. "I think he's involved in this somehow." Sam frowned and looked toward the windows. "He's involved in something over here in Spicetown. I don't know exactly what, but he's up to something."

Conrad clasped his hands in front of him on the desk. "Bobby called me yesterday."

Sam's eyebrows shot up.

"He asked questions about the case. I thought it was odd at the time because it was the type of thing he could pull from his own officer's reports. I couldn't understand why he was asking me."

"He called to talk to you about this case?" Sam's brow furrowed.

"No, he acted as though he was calling to express concerns about you working with Kimball."

Sam's tossed his hands up. "What?"

"I know." Conrad nodded. "It seemed lame to me at the time because he did that months ago. We've already discussed the topic, and the matter is closed. After I reiterated that, he started asking about your interviews. To be honest with you, I thought he was just worried about my involvement. I thought he was quizzing me to see if I was getting involved in the case or not." Conrad shrugged. "You know, wanting to see what I knew."

"Why would he care? He should be grateful if you're helping with this."

"Well..." Conrad winced. "Bobby and I have a history. I don't think he would particularly want me getting too involved in anything that belonged to him, although I have to admit, his mood has been more positive, more pleasing lately than it used to be."

"Gwen mentioned that to me, that you knew the sheriff before he was elected."

"Yes, we worked together years ago. We didn't get along well then either." Conrad chuckled. "So, what exactly do you mean by involved? Is that what makes you think this isn't an accident?"

Sam pointed at Conrad. "Exactly. The fact that he keeps making inquiries, asking who I'm interviewing, and showing so much interest is really odd."

"There could be a million reasons for that though. I don't know how he could be involved in something that looks like an accident."

"It's not just that. When I interviewed a couple of the miners yesterday, they asked about him."

"Hmm?" Conrad scowled.

"They asked if I worked directly for him and if I knew him. I told them yes, I worked for the Sheriff. I didn't explain anything else, but they just nodded. One of them even sort of smirked. It was weird."

"Who were these guys?"

"Noah Yates was the cocky one. I'd have to check my file for the other name."

"I don't know that name at all." Conrad wrote it down on his desk pad so he could ask Cora Mae.

"Both of those guys were new hires. They didn't seem to know anybody on the regular shift. They didn't even know the victim's husband."

"What made you interview them?"

"I just asked for all employees to come down to the station. After that we separated them by who lived in Miner's Meadow. Gwen interviewed those, and I took the rest. She asked them about seeing the victim walking Sunday morning. I focused more on the interpersonal relationships among the employees. I gathered enough to understand that most everyone pretty much hates Peter Jessup."

"Really! Why?"

"They think he's a snitch. He is constantly filing complaints and tattling on the other employees. I got the impression he is sort of a professional whistle blower."

"Oh, that will make you unpopular pretty quick." Conrad smiled.

"Yeah, last year he complained about some equipment needing maintenance and it shut the whole place down for a few weeks. No pay checks. Another time, one of his complaints canceled some overtime they were planning to work. He's got a lot of enemies."

"Any complaints about the wife?"

Sam shook his head. "The few that knew her only offered sympathy for her death, and sympathy because she was married to Peter." Sam grinned.

"Has the Sheriff ever mentioned the mine to you before? Maybe he has a friend or family member employed there. He might be concerned a scandal could close the mine down. I know it's not been doing well. I'm told that's why Walter Slope is here. They sent him to try to save it. Bad press won't help and closing it down at Christmas will devastate a lot of people."

"Maybe." Sam shrugged. "I asked him if he knew Noah Yates and he said he didn't. I have to say though, I've had a bad feeling about him for some time now. I just keep getting a vibe that there's something going on. Do you know what I mean? I can't put my finger on anything, but he's not being straight."

Conrad nodded. He'd had that niggling before, and Bobby Bell was capable of underhanded things but sharing Bobby's past with the present would catch up with him. He would be the one tarnished because Bobby knew how to fight back, and he didn't care who he took down. Conrad didn't make the same mistake twice.

"I do understand those feelings, but you're playing with fire. You can't touch him. Even with proof, he'll find a way to take you down with him. He has no conscience. I have to warn you to step away from that issue and just concentrate on the Jessup case. Looking back in my history with Bobby, I wish I'd taken that advice."

"You caught Bell at something? You turned him in?" Sam leaned forward with his elbows on his knees.

"I can't really get into it, but I can tell you that self-preservation is my best advice to you. You have to guard your career."

Sam looked down at the floor. "I understand."

"Just focus on your case and if Bell flops into the middle of it and falls on his face, your hands are clean!" Conrad held both of his hands up as if he were under arrest.

"Gotcha, Chief," Sam said with a snicker. "I better get back at it. I'll check in with you later."

"Okay. Holler if you need anything."

§

"Good morning, Mrs. Keslar." Jill Seabrook held

the front door open to the Irenic Wellness Center and ushered Grace in the door. "I'm glad you came by. All the flooring is done, and we received some equipment yesterday. Olivia and I have almost gotten all of it set up. Would you like to see it?"

"Yes, dear. I'm glad to hear that, but I really came because I wanted to see the roof repairs. They look nicely done. There is still some debris out back, but I guess we have to wait a little longer for someone to pick it up."

"Yes. It should all be gone by Monday." Jill stopped in the center of the lobby as Olivia walked out of the yoga room.

"Good morning," Olivia said timidly.

Grace nodded at Olivia. "Is the office furniture here yet?"

"Yes!" Jill pointed toward the office but noticed Grace did not turn to go check. "Would you like to see it?"

"No, that's fine. Are you happy with it?"

"It's very nice." Jill nodded. "The tables for the nutritional counseling arrived and the counters for the shop are here, but we haven't unboxed them yet."

"Splendid! It sounds like everything is moving along well. The only problem is the vandalism."

"The Sheriff came by yesterday and took a look at it. He said he would try and have someone drive by in the evenings to keep an eye on the place." Jill smiled. "I guess the officer you met with must have sent him his report."

"I had arrangements for a security system to be installed on the 28th, but I called them and told them it cannot wait. They will be out here tomorrow to run the wiring." Grace handed Jill a business card. "Here is the name and number."

Jill took the card and slipped it into her pocket after glancing at it.

"Until then, I'm going to pay someone to stay out here tonight and watch the place. I guess I'll go by the police department and see if I can hire an off-duty officer for the job. If not, I'll call a security firm in Paxton."

"I would hate to see someone break-in now that we have all this expensive equipment in the building." Jill turned around and looked out the window. "There isn't much traffic on this road at night."

"The vandalism is causing us delays, and it is just senseless. I can't let it continue."

"I can stay out here tonight, Mrs. Keslar." Olivia stepped forward when Jill looked at her in shock. "I don't mind."

"I don't know that it would be safe for you." Jill placed her hand over her heart. "What would you do if someone showed up and started breaking a window?"

"Jill is right. You may not be—"

"I can ask my boyfriend to stay out here with me. Surely with two of us, we will be fine."

Grace's forehead creased as she hummed. "Okay. I guess that would be okay. Just make certain you keep everything locked up and call the Spicetown Police if something happens. They are much closer than the sheriff's department."

"Oh, I will Mrs. Keslar." Olivia smiled. "Thank you!"

Chapter 15

"Good morning, Walter," Cora Mae said when she answered her cell phone and felt her cheeks heat. "How are you today?"

"Good morning! Well, I'm having a very unusual day. That's why I called. I thought maybe you would know something about what was going on out here and could possibly help me."

"At the mine?"

"Yes. There is an officer out here from the Spicetown Police Department and a detective from the Sheriff's Department. Which one is working this case?"

"Well, it's a collaborative effort as I understand it." Cora Mae sighed. "Spicetown frequently—"

"And is this even a case? I thought everyone said she fell and hit her head. They are causing chaos out here, stopping productivity, and I'm not sure why. Has something happened that has changed things? Have you heard anything about this?"

"I heard that you were expected at the police

department yesterday and you didn't show. They were—"

"I don't know why they were expecting me to do anything! I don't have anything to do with all this and no one told me to come down there."

"You just need to give them your statement. I think they need a statement from all the mine employees due to the location of the—"

"Well, I don't appreciate that they are trying to drag the mine into all of this. It's casting a disparaging gloom over our contribution to this community."

"They are just doing their job, Walter."

"They are damaging our reputation needlessly and on behalf of the mine, I wish to file a formal complaint. Do I have the correct department for that?"

Cora Mae's heart was pounding. "I believe you have, Mr. Slope. Your concerns have been noted. Have a good day." Cora tapped the large circle to disconnect the call and saw her hand quiver. Whether it was from anger, shock, or hurt feelings, she wasn't certain.

"Mayor, Mrs. Keslar is here to see you." Cora nodded to Amanda to invite her in.

Standing, she took a deep breath to clear her head. "Good morning, Mrs. Keslar. How lovely to see you today! Are you doing some Christmas shopping in town?"

"Good morning, Mayor. No, I'm out running some last-minute errands and realized I hadn't been by City Hall. Your Christmas decorations are wonderful this year. You've added some new items. I love the garland around the counter."

"Thank you!" Cora's cell phone rang. Walter was calling back, and she pushed the button to silence the sound. "I'm sorry. We did buy a few new items this year. The biggest difference is the decorators. Nellie and Tommy Turner came by to decorate the tree for us and they do such a fabulous job."

"That's wonderful!" Grace tossed her hand in the air. "I could have used their help this year! I will remember and hire them next year myself."

"I think they enjoy it. They do the Christmas tree at the police department also and help at the Community Center." Cora Mae sat down at her desk and glanced at the voice mail notification on her cell phone.

"There are so many trees in town." Grace smiled. "It's a wonderful time of year."

Cora Mae nodded.

"The reason I stopped in was to make certain you had heard about my party. I hope you can come out to my house this weekend. I don't mail invitations. I prefer just to invite everyone, but I hadn't seen you in weeks."

"Yes, we've been missing each other, but I had heard about it, and I'd love to come." Cora had already been invited by Conrad and Walter but did not feel right attending if Grace wasn't going to invite her.

"Everyone is welcome. We'll have food and music. I'm celebrating more than just the holiday this year. I have a new business venture that starts January second. I'm very excited about it."

"I've heard about that as well and I'm very interested to learn more. During the summer months, I was getting regular exercise by walking around town. That worked well in the spring, summer and fall, but the weather is just too cold now. I've tried and I just can't get myself out the door with these temperatures. I was hoping your new facility would offer an easy exercise option for me."

"We definitely will be doing just that! There will be sessions offered that I'm sure will be just what you're looking for. I'm so excited about this new chapter. We've had so many little glitches lately that I've been getting discouraged, but I'm hoping we have that all straightened out now."

"Glitches?" Cora stood and walked around her desk since Grace had never taken a seat.

"Yes, we've had some vandals and some unfortunate accidents that I never expected. I'm getting a security system installed this week, and until then, I've just posted someone out there at all times. I don't know what else to do. I never thought we would have problems like this, but I guess we are just too far outside of town."

"There isn't a lot of traffic out that way." Cora frowned. "I wouldn't have thought anyone would take much notice either."

"Someone has." Grace chuckled. "We haven't given up yet though. We have gotten the hole in the roof fixed this week and I have an employee who is spending the night out there to keep an eye on things.

"Hole in the roof?" Cora gasped. "What caused that?"

"No idea. Something busted a hole through our new roof, and we have to wait on the carpenter to repair the damage in the attic. A freak accident, I suppose."

Cora scowled. "You have filed police reports?"

"Ah, yes. London has been very prompt and

helpful. We will keep moving forward." Grace walked to the door and waved over her shoulder. "I will see you this weekend, Mayor. Don't work too hard."

"Have a good day." Cora Mae shook her head. An odd bird, but a kind heart. She could hear her in the outer office inviting Amanda and Bryan to her party. It wouldn't surprise her if the entire lobby had already been invited also.

Cora picked up her phone and glanced at the voice mail notification. She wasn't ready to listen to that yet. She did not want to hear anything from Walter except an apology and frankly, she wasn't ready for an apology yet either.

§

"Sorry, Chief." Detective Sam Snell sighed. "I never thought I'd be stuck out at the mine all day. This should have been really easy, in and out, but it's not turning out that way. Do you need Officer Kimball to come back to the office? I feel bad I've tied her up, too."

"Nah, Sam. It's okay. I just didn't know what to do with these folks that are showing up. I just needed to know your plan. We've got the husband and boyfriend coming in at the same time. I don't want to risk a brawl in my lobby." Conrad chuckled. "I put one of them in a room. Do you want me to go ahead and get what I can? From your reports, I think I know what you need from them."

"Yeah, Chief. That would be swell if you could do that. They both have a period of time we need to account for, and I just left them a voice mail message to drop in the PD. I never thought about them showing up at the same time."

"Sometimes when they come at the same time, those situations are actually helpful. It might make each of them talk a little better knowing the other one is here." Conrad winked at Briscoe who popped his head up off the dog bed when he heard Conrad say, 'come'. Seeing it wasn't directed at him, he relaxed.

"What's the trouble at the mine? Why is it taking so long?"

"The manager, Walter Slope, is making a big fuss of everything. He's notified the union. They showed up to protest our interviewing staff during work hours. Mr. Slope keeps saying we're hurting his production, but I explained to him that all of these guys were supposed to be at the station on Monday. They didn't show and so they are the reason for the problem, not us."

"He didn't show up either." Conrad scowled.

"I reminded him of that, but he insists that none of this applies to him. He doesn't even know the woman and wasn't in the vicinity during the time period. He's just decided to rule himself out!"

Conrad chuckled. "I'd make his interview last the longest."

Sam laughed. "See you later, Chief, and thanks for your help."

Chapter 16

Conrad hung up the phone and decided to start with Trevor Mason. He had the victim's husband, Peter Jessup in an interview room already, but he would keep. Walking down to dispatch, he waited for Georgia Marks to end her phone call and to let her know his plans before escorting Trevor into another interview room.

"Mr. Mason," Conrad said as he motioned toward the table and chairs. "Have a seat for me, please. I'm Chief Harris. I don't believe we've met, but I did see you out at the scene. I understand you reported Jane missing."

"I did. I already gave the other guy a statement on that." Trevor put his elbows on the table to clasp his hands in front of him.

"Yes, but based on some other reports, we are missing a little bit in your timeline for that morning. Can we start again?"

"Sure." Trevor shrugged his shoulders.

"Let's start with Sunday morning. Where were you

when you woke up that morning?"

"At home! Where else would I be?"

"Do you live alone? Was anyone else at your home when you woke up?"

"Are you asking if I had an alibi?" Trevor splayed his hands on the table and leaned forward.

"No, I'm asking if there was anyone else at your home when you woke up Sunday morning." Conrad sat down across from Trevor and crossed his ankle up over his knee.

"No. I live alone. There was nobody there." Trevor looked down at the floor.

"What time was it?"

"Around seven o'clock, I think." Trevor shrugged. "I got up and took a shower to get ready for church."

"Did you talk to Jane that morning? Did you send or receive a text or call from her?" Conrad knew he had sent a text to Jane's phone a little before nine o'clock, but Jane had not responded.

"I texted her, but she didn't answer. I had invited her to church many times, but she had finally agreed to meet me. I sent her a text to remind her and tell her I would wait on her in the parking lot."

"No answer?" Conrad raised his eyebrows.

"No. She didn't reply. She had backed out on me before though, so I wasn't surprised."

"Where did you go after you left the church?"

"Home."

Conrad nodded. "What did you do at home?"

"Changed my clothes. I tried to call Jane and see if she wanted to get lunch. She didn't answer, so I made myself a sandwich."

"At what point did you decide she was missing?"

Trevor clasped his hands on the table again and

tightened his grip until his fingertips dug into the back of his hand. “After I ate. I got concerned about her not responding. That’s not like her. She goes for those walks in the woods, but she always goes home by noon.”

“Did you think she might be with her husband?” Conrad held his hands out. “Or maybe she didn’t want to respond because she had changed her mind about meeting you?”

“Peter? No, she would never be with Peter, and it was no big deal that she didn’t show. I invite her all the time and she doesn’t show up.”

“Has she ever gone to church with you?” Conrad lifted one eyebrow.

“Not on a Sunday morning. I got her to go to a Bible Study meeting once. I think she wants to be involved. She’s just afraid for some reason.”

“Maybe she’s concerned about being seen out with another man? She is a married woman.” Conrad folded his arms across his chest.

“Nah, it’s not like that. Everybody tries to make it something sinister. Jane and I were just friends.”

Conrad hummed. “You said she would never be with Peter. She did live with him. Correct? She was married to him.”

“Yeah, but they just share a house now. She stayed because she really didn’t have anywhere to go, and they were in debt too much to split up. It was kind of like being separated and having a roommate. They had separate bedrooms. Peter didn’t want to live with his mom, so they just...” Trevor shrugged his shoulders.

“Aren’t you currently married, Mr. Mason?”

“Technically, yes, but we’re separated.” Trevor

shook his head.

"You did recently have a girlfriend, though. Correct?"

"I went out with Lindsey Thurman a few times, if that's what you're talking about. I wouldn't call that having a girlfriend. She goes to my church, and I work with her brother. It wasn't serious."

"You also work with Jane's husband, Peter. Are you two friends?"

"No, just coworkers." Trevor looked at the wall away from the door. "Nobody really gets along very well with Peter."

"Why is that?" Conrad planted his feet on the floor and leaned on his elbows.

"He's just a troublemaker. Always telling on everybody, complaining about everything. I can't believe they even keep him around."

"Okay, so let's go back to where we were." Conrad took a deep breath. "You finished lunch and then became concerned about Jane."

"That's right." Trevor nodded vigorously and leaned forward.

"Is that when you called the Sheriff's Department?" Conrad leaned back in his chair. The call regarding Jane was not received until late in the afternoon.

"No." Trevor's eyes fell again, and Conrad waited to see if he would continue on his own. "That's when I went out looking for her."

"Walk me through that," Conrad said as he relaxed back into his chair. "Where did you go first?"

Trevor began to run his thumbnail around each of his other nails and fidget in his chair. "I, uh, drove by the house first."

Conrad nodded.

"Her car was there, but she usually walked."

"Was her husband's car there?" Conrad dropped his head to catch Trevor's gaze.

"No."

"Would you have stopped if it had been?" Conrad leaned into the table and forced Trevor to make eye contact.

"Uh, maybe. I mean Peter knew we were friends. I probably wouldn't have that day because I was just trying to make sure she was okay. You know, so I would have thought if he's home, that she's all right, but..."

"You wouldn't have stopped Sunday, but it would have put your mind at ease." Conrad raised his eyebrows seeking concurrence.

"Yeah. Yeah. I could have let it go, but I went up to the house and rang the bell. She didn't answer."

This was the discrepancy Sam had been concerned with. Trevor had not mentioned this step in his original statement, but neighbors in Miner's Meadow had seen him at Jane's door. "Okay, then what?"

"I drove down to the woods. I knew she always entered off the blacktop road behind the mine. Problem is, she could go any direction from there."

"So, what did you do?" Conrad would have tried calling her phone if it had been him. He thought it odd that Trevor had not called more than he did. He would have tried to hear the phone ring in the woods. In fact, the officers the night of the search had tried that repeatedly. Even a silenced phone usually vibrates, and Briscoe will hear it.

"I yelled for her. I walked in the main path entrance about fifty feet, but I never heard anything.

She didn't respond. It was dead quiet out there. I felt like she would have heard me if she had been in there somewhere."

"So, help me understand where your head was." Conrad scooted his chair closer to the table. "Her car is at home. She's got to be on foot or with someone. Right?"

"Yeah." Trevor nodded.

"She's not at home and you think she's not in the woods. Where do you go from there?"

Trevor stared at his thumbnail and picked at the cuticle. "I drove around a little."

Conrad waited.

"I drove further down the mine road, drove through the subdivision, any place I thought she might walk. I drove over to her mother-in-law's house—"

"Is that within walking distance? Would Jane have walked there?" It was not, but Conrad wondered why Trevor would go there.

"No, but I thought maybe she went over there with Peter. Maybe they were both in his car." Trevor met Conrad's gaze. "It could have been her birthday or something. I didn't know."

"I see." Conrad nodded. It was a stretch, but it did show the door still open to a married couple. "What was your next thought? Does she have girlfriends that she might have gone somewhere with?"

"Why are we going over all this? We know where she was. These are questions that should have been asked Sunday. Not now!"

"Let me be honest with you, Trevor." Conrad leaned back and scrutinized the nervous young man across from him. "We have reports from others regarding your whereabouts that afternoon and we are just trying to piece them all together. We need a clear timeline of the different places you went that afternoon, so we can reconcile the statement from others that were interviewed. Each time we talk to you, we hear something new.

"Now, this is not a Spicetown case and so I am just assisting in this investigation, but I can tell you that from my experience and from my perspective, that behavior signals someone has a secret they are trying to keep. Keeping secrets around a time period where a suspicious death has occurred is never a good practice. My advice to you is that whatever you are trying to keep quiet is not nearly as important as being straight forward about what you did on Sunday."

Trevor took a deep breath and sat up straighter in his chair. "I'm not leaving anything out that involves Jane."

"So, you went other places that afternoon, that don't involve Jane?" Conrad tossed his hands open in a suggestive gesture. "Places you don't want to mention?"

"No!" Trevor shook his head. "I don't mean that. I don't really remember every little detail. I drove around. I was trying to think. I didn't know what to do. I thought I should call the police, but they always say the police won't do anything until someone is missing for days. I even thought about calling Peter to see if he knew anything, but it's just weird between us and I didn't see that going well. I was driving around thinking about all these things and I don't know every street I took so maybe lots of people saw me." Trevor shrugged his shoulders.

"Okay, take a breath. Tell me about Jane's photography. What exactly was she photographing out there? Birds? Trees?" Conrad shook his head in bewilderment.

"Yeah, nature. Sometimes in the winter she shot with black and white film. She knew how to get the light just right and she was good at it."

"Did she ever photograph people?"

Trevor frowned. "You mean like family portraits?"

Conrad shrugged.

"No, not that I know of." Trevor shook his head.

"You mentioned that Jane and Peter had financial challenges, I just thought that might be something she could do on the side to make extra money."

"All of the miners have money problems." Trevor huffed. "It just goes with the territory."

"Are you including yourself in that?" Conrad smiled.

Trevor just hunched his shoulders and looked away. "She sold some of her pictures. I don't know what kind of money that pays. I think she did it because she enjoyed it."

"I would guess that camera is pretty expensive."

"Oh, yeah!" Trevor's eyes grew large. "She took care of that thing like it was her baby." Trevor smiled.

"She wouldn't put it down and forget about it or leave it anywhere by accident." Conrad nodded.

"No! Even when it was around her neck, she had her hands on it." Trevor's gaze rose up over Conrad's head.

"So, it is odd that they found her camera almost a quarter of a mile from where her body was." Conrad nodded briskly and rose from his chair. "If you don't mind, I've got to step out for a minute, but I'll be back shortly."

Turning to leave, Conrad caught the shocked expression on Trevor's face. It seemed genuine.

Sheri Richey

Chapter 17

"Peter! Good to see you again." Conrad stretched out his hand to shake Peter Jessup's hand and then motioned for him to sit across the table from him. "I'm sorry to keep you waiting, but I thought maybe Detective Snell would be coming in soon. I talked to him on the phone, and he's tied up this morning."

"Oh, I can come back another time." Peter stood and started to walk around the table.

"No. No need. He told me what he needed and I'm going to take care of it for him. Have a seat. It'll just take a minute."

"Oh, okay. Thanks, Chief. What does he need?"

Conrad pulled out a chair and turned it around to straddle it. "I'm sure you know he is getting lots of statements from different people and sometimes those little details overlap or don't line up quite right. Then he has to narrow down what the problem is, so the timeline is clear."

"Sure, Chief." Peter nodded. "Makes sense."

"Okay. Well, the first little hiccup he encountered

was Sunday morning. You said you were at your girlfriend's house all morning, spent the night and was there when you got the call that Jane was missing."

"She's not really my girlfriend, uh—"

"No judgment here." Conrad waved a dismissive hand. "We just had a report that you were not at her home the entire time. Can you fill us in on that?"

Peter frowned and took a deep breath. "Uh, I just ran out for a minute that morning for some breakfast. Olivia sleeps late and I was hungry."

"Oh, okay." Conrad pushed his chair back and stretched his legs out. "What did you get?"

"What?" Peter's head jerked back to meet Conrad's gaze.

"What did you get to eat?"

"Oh, I just ran into the gas station down the road. Grabbed some coffee and a fruit pie. I needed to put gas in my car anyway."

"Okay," Conrad nodded. So far, so good. His visit to the gas station had been reported by one of his neighbors. "Then what?"

"I went back to Olivia's." Peter's eyes widened innocently.

"Did you take the food back there? Eat after you arrived?" Conrad stretched out his neck and tried to encourage Peter to continue.

"I ate in the car at the gas station." Peter smiled. "It was gone in a couple of bites."

"Remind me again. Where is Olivia's apartment?" Conrad squinted one eye and hoped Peter would volunteer his route. It was so much easier when people were honest.

"On Clover Road."

"So, you went to the gas station on Clover Road." Conrad nodded, hoping Peter would correct him.

"No. I went to the gas station on the blacktop road. I always go there. I have a loyalty card, so I get a discount."

"Ah," Conrad nodded. "So, you drove a couple of miles for gas and breakfast?"

"Yeah. I had time to kill, and Olivia sleeps late. I'm kind of addicted to these little fruit pies. I get them on my way to work a lot."

Conrad chuckled. "I understand. So, you weren't on the mine road that morning?"

"What?"

"Someone said they saw you on the mine road." Conrad shrugged. "I know that's pretty close to your house and the gas station. Did you actually drive down that road?"

"Who saw me?"

"Oh, I don't rightly know." Conrad tugged at his waistband to reposition his belt. I just know the detective had a little hiccup with that and we need to straighten it out some. Trying to get the timeline right."

"Yeah." Peter's gaze went off to the wall on the left. "I drove down there, but I just turned around. I was just looking around. I wanted to see if anything was going on out there."

"On a Sunday! Do they work out there sometimes on a Sunday?"

"Not the regular staff, but stuff goes on out there sometimes, stuff they don't want us to know about."

"Ah, so you were playing the watchdog. Huh?"

"Yeah, exactly. If you don't keep your eye on those guys, they take advantage."

Conrad frowned. "Do you mean your coworkers?" It was a coworker that reported seeing him turn out of the mine road entrance mid-morning on Sunday.

"Nah, not so much. It's corporate. That's when they move stuff, the days when we aren't around to see."

"Hmm, I don't know much about work out at the mine. Can't say I'm that clear on what you all do." Conrad smiled.

"It's dangerous work and there are safety precautions that need to be followed. They'll take shortcuts sometimes if they can."

"I know there's been some changes out there recently. You got a new boss, and he's closing tunnels to try to improve profits."

"Slope, yeah. He's got some different ideas, but you can't trust any of them." Peter scowled.

"Sounds like you are kind of a whistleblower of sorts. You keep an eye on things for your coworkers' safety. I'm sure they appreciate that."

"They should." Peter nodded.

"Okay, so you drove out there and turned around. Right? You didn't stop or see anyone out there?"

"Jane wouldn't have been that far up. She walked in the woods behind the mine property, but she wouldn't have been interested in going that far back. She didn't go down the mine road."

"I think the detective just needed to line up the statements, and we didn't have you driving down that way in your first statement."

"Oh, okay." Peter brushed imaginary lint front his shirt.

"One last thing, Peter. I'm just curious. I know you and Jane were not talking a lot from day to day, but if the police hadn't gotten involved and things hadn't unfolded the way they have, when would you have missed her?"

"I'm sorry?"

"When would you have stopped and thought: Where's Jane? When would you have called the police?"

"Uh, I don't know." Peter looked down at the table.

"Would you have come home Sunday evening or night? Would you have been worried if she had not been home? If so, who would you call first about it?"

"Uh, I guess I would have gotten worried if she wasn't home by like ten o'clock Sunday night. She usually goes to bed about that time."

"Even with her car in the drive?" Conrad squinted. "Does she leave with other people sometimes? Could someone have picked her up?"

"I guess so. I don't really know. I probably wouldn't have thought about it until it was late. Then I would have wondered if there was something wrong."

"And what would you have done about it? Does she have a friend you would have called first? Or would you have just called the police?"

"I don't know. I might just have gone on to bed and figured it really wasn't any of my business."

"Okay," Conrad stood up. "Thank you for your help, Peter. I'll let Detective Snell know and he can call you if he needs anything else. Conrad patted him on the back as he walked around the table toward the door. Following him out, he just had to shake his head.

§

"I'm glad you got your invitation."

Cora Mae had mentioned earlier to Amanda that she had not been invited to the Christmas party yet. "It sounds rather informal. She said everyone is invited."

"Are you going with Mr. Slope?" Amanda scrunched up her shoulders bashfully.

"I think I will do best to accompany myself," Cora said sternly, then regretted letting her frustration with Walter color her response. The voice message apology had been adequate, but it did not absolve him of wrongdoing, and it was all too telling of a personality flaw she could not tolerate.

"What are you wearing?" Amanda grimaced. "Bryan thinks we should go because it's good for business. He hates that kind of stuff though and he'll probably hide behind me all night."

Cora Mae laughed. "I have a Christmas jacket that I'm going to wear. I can't pass up an opportunity to use it when I can."

"Mrs. Keslar makes me nervous." Amanda shrugged. "I don't know why. She's unpredictable and I'm always afraid I'm going to become a target of her attention."

"Does Bryan know her?"

"No, that's the thing, he's never met her. He will freak out if she decides to give him another name or tell him one of her stories about the war."

Cora grinned. "I think it's innocent enough. Eccentricity can be charming."

"I ran into Kassie Jackson at the grocery store this weekend. Do you remember her?"

"I do."

"Well, she's just started working for Mrs. Keslar and she said she's been renamed as Alice." Amanda chuckled. "She just laughed about it. She thinks Mrs. Keslar is fun, but one of the other girls she hired is a little freaked out."

"What is Kassie doing for her?"

"Housecleaning. You know she's offering her home to people who need lodging for the spa. I guess it will be a bed and breakfast type of place."

"Yes," Cora said. "I've wondered if that will harm the Nutmeg Inn. They are full during holidays, but they almost always have rooms otherwise. I wouldn't think that the spa would draw that much long-distance interest."

"It sounds like an elaborate place, so it might. I'm wondering if the locals will want to go. From what I hear, it's got to be pricey."

"Something to look forward to in the new year!"

Sheri Richey

Chapter 18

"This is crazy," Peter Jessup whispered to Olivia as she locked the glass entrance doors to the Irenic Wellness Center behind him.

"There's no need to whisper. We're the only ones here, silly." Olivia D'Asaro chuckled.

"Are you sure this is all right? They know I'm here?" Peter rubbed his hands together to warm up and looked around before taking a step away from the door.

"Yes! Mrs. Keslar knows I'm staying out here all night, and I told her I would have my boyfriend with me. She didn't want me to be alone."

Peter frowned. "It's creepy out here."

"Not in the daytime. Follow me. I've got all the lights on in the back and it's not scary in there. I brought games and snacks. Jill even loaned me her little television from her office. We're going to have a great slumber party!"

Olivia snatched the pizza box from Peter's hands. "I'm starved."

"Do you have plates?" Peter looked around the yoga room. "I don't see any chairs."

"We can sit on the floor. Here," Olivia pointed to a padded floor mat. "Best seat in the house! We can see out the front in case someone pulls in, but no one can see us."

"This feels weird." Peter slipped his coat off. "Just being in here at night is eerie. What do you do out here? The place is half empty."

"After we eat, I'll give you a tour. Each room has a different purpose. There is one for yoga, one for spin class, one for the sauna and massage, one for nutritional consults—"

"Okay. Okay, I get it. What's this big circle in the center for?"

"This is the waiting room for people that come with appointments. In the daytime, it's really pretty out here. There's colored glass in the skylights." Olivia pointed to the domed ceiling in the center.

"Do you make the appointments?"

"I probably will sometimes, but I'm the manager's assistant, so I do whatever she needs. Since we aren't open yet, I don't know what it will be like, but she seems okay."

"Give me another slice." Peter pointed at the pizza box.

"How did your interview go today?"

"At the police department? It was fine. Somebody just told them that they saw me near the mine on Sunday and they wanted to know why."

"Sunday? When were you at the mine?"

"When I went to get gas, before you got up. I was just driving around and wanted to take a look. It was nothing."

"They called me this afternoon." Olivia wiped her hands on a napkin. "They wanted me to come down and make a statement, but I told them I have to work. If they want it that bad, they can come down here."

"You better go down there," Peter scolded. "You don't want—"

"They can come out here. This is a new job. I'm not going to ask for time off for that. It's silly anyway. I didn't even know her, and I was home all morning."

"Yeah, but they probably want to ask questions about me. You need to tell them I was at your house all night until the police called the next day."

"One of the officers was out here already about the roof damage and he didn't say a thing to me."

"Was that Detective Snell?"

"No, some guy named London. Mrs. Keslar knows him."

"I don't know him. I don't think he's on this case. I talked to Chief Harris today."

"Somebody just pulled in the parking lot." Olivia scrambled up to her feet and went to the windows. "It looks like a truck."

"Call the police." Peter put his drink down and tossed his plate in the pizza box.

"Maybe they're just turning around." Olivia walked around Peter and went into the yoga room where there were more windows. "They just went around back."

"Are they turning around?" Peter followed her into the room. "Don't let them see you."

"They can't see in. These windows have a dark tint and without the lights on in the room, I don't think they can't see us."

"Do you know the truck? Maybe it's a workman

that was here during the day and he forgot something."

"It's just a white truck. They all look alike." Olivia walked to the other end of the room. "He's getting out of the truck."

Peter followed behind her. "It looks like he's waiting on someone. He's just leaning on the truck. He's not coming toward the building. Maybe it's nothing."

"Our cars are out front. You'd think he would be worried someone was inside."

"I guess not. Here comes another car." Peter pointed over her shoulder. "He is meeting someone."

When the vehicle turned around the corner of the building, they both saw the reflective stripe at the same time.

"It's the police."

Peter sighed. "Maybe he's getting pulled over and he just came into the parking lot to get off the road. Nothing to worry about if they are already on it. I wonder if someone isn't watching the place since Mrs. Keslar reported the vandalism. Is it that London guy?"

"I don't know. I can't see." Olivia stood on her tiptoes.

"The cop is getting out of the car, but the other guy doesn't look like he's in trouble or anything. They're just chatting." Peter moved around Olivia to the other side. "I always thought they made you stay in the car."

"He's smiling." Olivia pointed out the window. "They know each other. I guess it's nothing." Olivia stepped back. "I'm going to finish eating."

Peter stayed behind for a little bit, but the two men just continued to lean against their vehicle and chat.

Finally, he went back to the center of the building.

"There's one more piece," Peter said. "I'll split it with you."

"No, that's okay. I'm full. You can have it." Olivia took a deep breath. "I should go get on the bike now and work off all of that pizza. That room over there is for spin class." Olivia pointed. "They were hard to put together." A small squeak escaped from Olivia's lips as she jumped from the sound of someone knocking on the front glass door. Not knocking with their knuckles but rapping something hard against the glass.

Peter tossed his plate again and headed toward the front.

"No, don't go out there. They'll see you. Those windows aren't tinted, and that's why I didn't turn on the front lights. Come in Jill's office. We can see out her windows." Olivia pinched the sleeve of Peter's shirt and pulled him with her.

Posing in the corner, they both peered out. The policeman had rapped the glass with the end of his long flashlight and was now shining a beam through the door.

"We should go let him inside." Peter stepped back away from the window.

"No! We don't know him," Olivia said.

"He's probably just worried about the cars outside and wants to make sure we're okay. He's the police, for goodness sakes!"

"I'm calling the Spicetown Police. That's what Mrs. Keslar told me to do." Olivia pulled out her cell phone.

Peter shook his head. "That's crazy. The guy at the door is—"

Olivia held her hand up with her palm facing Peter. "Hi, this is Olivia D'Asaro and I'm out at the Irenic Wellness Center. Some guy in a white truck and another guy in a sheriff's car are outside. One of them is banging on my front door, but I'm afraid to open the door. The other guy is around back. We've had some vandalism out here and Mrs. Keslar filled a report with Officer London. She told me to call you guys if anything happened out here tonight."

Peter stepped back as the officer walked by the window they were standing nearby. "Are you sure he can't see us?"

Olivia nodded. "Okay. Thanks." Olivia pocketed her cell phone and peeked out the window again. "They're sending someone out here. He said someone was close by. They don't know who these people are either."

Peter walked back to the center and headed for the yoga room in the back of the building. "Is the other guy still here?"

Olivia stayed at the front window in Jill's office watching for the police but yelled back at Peter. "Do you see him?"

"Olivia!" Peter scurried into Jill's office. "That guy is pulling the siding off the back of the building with a crowbar!"

"What?" Olivia left her post at Jill's front window to go run to the yoga room to confirm. Grabbing her cell phone again, she tried to get her phone to record what she saw from the window although she wasn't sure it would film well in the dark.

"Another cop just pulled in!" Peter rushed back to the yoga room to tell Olivia. "He should be coming around the back. The cop in the front waved at him, but he drove around the building." Peter pointed. "There he is."

The police car made a ninety degree turn and pointed his headlights at the young man with the crowbar and hit his siren for just a second.

"Holy cow!" Olivia gasped. "He's arresting him!"

"Where's the other cop?" Peter looked up and saw the other guy walk around the corner of the building.

"It looks like he is trying to stop the Spicetown cop from taking him. Aren't you glad we didn't open the door? Something's not right."

Peter stepped away from the window again, flinching each time the cop looked his way. "They're leaving."

As the sheriff's car left with the other man in the back of the squad car, the Spicetown policeman returned to his car.

"I guess all the excitement is over." Olivia shrugged and turned to walk out of the yoga room.

"Do you think we need to stay the rest of the night?" Peter followed her.

"I'm afraid to leave. I promised Mrs. Keslar I would watch the place and somebody else might show up." Olivia sat down on the mat and began collecting the paper towels and wrappers from their dinner and drinks. "I wish I knew what happened out there. Do you think that cop is going to sit there all night?"

Peter jumped when they heard rapping on the front glass door again. "Is that guy back?"

Olivia looked in Jill's office. "No, it's the Spicetown policeman."

"Should we answer the door?"

Olivia's cell phone began to ring, and she looked at Peter as she stabbed the button on the display.

"Hello?"

Peter held his hands out and whispered, "Who is it?"

Olivia smiled and opened the door to the foyer. "Okay. Yes, I see him. Thank you."

Peter grabbed at the back of her shirt. "Was the cop calling you?"

"It was the police station. They asked me to let him in." Olivia turned the lock on the front door and Officer Harold "Wink" Hobson smiled.

"Evening, folks. Are you doing all right?"

Peter took a deep breath. This ordeal had been exhausting.

"Yes, thank you. I'm sorry if we weren't supposed to call, but Mrs. Keslar, the lady that owns this place, told me to call the Spicetown police if anything happened."

"That's just fine. I'm glad you did. My name is Officer Hobson. I just wanted to make sure you were okay before I left. Are you planning to stay the rest of the evening?"

Olivia looked at Peter. "Yes, I think I better. Mrs. Keslar would want me to stay."

"That's fine. You just call us if you need anything. Have a good evening."

Wink strolled to his squad car and waved as he pulled out of the parking lot.

Chapter 19

Conrad sat down heavily in his office chair and rocked it back on its springs until they creaked. "Back up, Wink. You pulled in and saw the sheriff's office squad car in the back of the building?"

"Yeah, my headlights hit Bobby first when I pulled in. He was waving his arms, but I drove around back because the call was some strange guy in a truck around the back."

"So, you ignored the Sheriff?" Conrad snickered. Bobby would probably make Wink pay for that eventually. "I didn't know it was Bobby at first. I just knew it was a county uniform."

"Okay, so you go around the back and see the guy pulling off the siding."

"Right. I get out, tell him to drop the crowbar and as I turn him around to cuff him, Bobby comes running around the side of the building."

"Did he say he knew the guy? Did the guy say anything at all?"

"No. Bobby just said 'I got this' and grabbed the

guy's arm. He pulled him away from me and pushed him in his own car. Not much I can do at that point. He has jurisdiction, and he is the almighty Sheriff after all." Wink rolled his eyes. "After he pulled away, I checked on the kids inside. They seemed fine. They were just watching the place for Mrs. Keslar."

"You don't know the guy's name?"

"Didn't get that far!"

"Good morning, Chief." Dispatch officer Georgia Marks leaned around the door frame. "I've got Sheriff Bell on the phone."

Conrad glanced at Wink and then back at Georgia. "Put him through."

Wink shut the office door and took a seat, but Conrad couldn't trust him to remain silent, so he didn't answer with the speaker button.

"Morning, Sheriff!" Conrad smiled at Wink and picked up his pencil to doodle while Bobby Bell began to weave his story.

"Morning, Connie. Just wanted to head you off early and let you know we appreciate all the help you're giving us with the Jessup case. I know you did some interviews for us yesterday."

"Yeah, Detective Snell got tied up at the mine, so I talked to a couple of people. It was not a problem at all. Happy to help."

"Very commendable. Just wanted to let you know your assistance doesn't go unnoticed. I saw another of your officers last night helping out with a call that should have been ours to take. We can't be everywhere all the time though and it's good to know that the Spicetown officers have got our back."

Conrad felt a slight tickle in the back of his throat that toyed with activating his gag reflex. "We try to keep up our end of things. The folks out at the new Wellness Center have been having some problems with vandals, so we have that road on patrol. What did you end up charging the guy with? Was there much damage?"

Bobby Bell sputtered a bit and muttered as if talking to someone else in the room. "I don't know the details. I handed it off, but you can trust it was taken care of."

"Sure thing, Sheriff. You have a good day."

"You too, Connie."

Conrad hung up the phone and inhaled while he stretched his arms over his head. Wishing he had put it on speaker phone just to have had a witness, he chuckled. "He didn't answer me, but I know him well enough to know he's already cut the guy lose. Did the truck stay at the center all night?"

"I don't know. The kids didn't call back in, so I assumed there was no more activity out there. I did call the plate into dispatch after the sheriff took him away though. It's all in my report."

"You go get some sleep. We'll check it out and see if it's gone. I want to get some pictures of the damage before Mrs. Keslar finds out what happened. Then I'm going to tell her to give Bobby a call."

Wink smiled and grabbed his coat.

"Hey, Georgie," Conrad yelled down the hallway. "Is London available?"

Wink busted out laughing as he pushed through the side door of the police station.

§

"Good morning, Walter." Cora Mae answered her

cell phone reluctantly, because she didn't want another voice mail.

"Cora Mae, I know you're still mad at me. I understand that, and I wouldn't be calling if I had another option, but—"

"What do you need, Walter?" Cora tried to sound patient, and she wanted to be patient, but Walter could be so dramatic. She just wasn't up to a performance today.

"Well, what do you have on your plate today? Are you going to be in the office or—"

"I am headed to the library in about twenty minutes. I'm on the Library Board and we have a Christmas function this morning. I have another obligation outside the office this afternoon as well."

"I was wondering if you could pick me up at the dentist this afternoon and give me a ride home."

"How are you planning to get to the dentist?"

"Oh, I can walk over there. It's right downtown, but I'm not sure I'll feel like walking back."

"You've already seen the dentist?"

"Yeah, I went when my tooth was hurting. They gave me antibiotic to stop that, but now I have to go back in. They won't let me drive home after the procedure and I just don't have anyone here I can ask. I can't ask my employees for help."

"What procedure?"

"They are pulling the tooth for me today."

"Oh," Cora Mae winced. "Have you had that done before?"

"Never. Have you?"

"I have. It's not one of my fondest memories." Cora touched her cheek.

"Is it really bad? I'd be lying if I said I wasn't a

little bit worried about it."

"I was worried, too. In fact, I think the anxiety of it was worse than the actual event," Cora Mae said. "Did they say what kind of anesthesia they would use?"

"They said I would have an IV of something and they asked me a bunch of questions about whether I had any problems with anxiety." Walter laughed nervously. "I didn't have until they started asking all of those questions."

"Don't let them get in your head. You just need to relax and let them do what they do. They're very experienced and I'm sure you won't have any difficulties. They'll give you some pain medication and you'll probably sleep well tonight."

"The play opens tonight and I'm going to miss it."

"Oh no! That's a shame. They have someone to stand in for you?"

"They do. I should be okay for tomorrow night's performance, but the dentist said I probably wouldn't feel like it tonight."

"That's disappointing."

"I know. I was looking forward to it, but if I don't do it now, it'll be next month before I can get another appointment with the holidays coming."

"I think I hear Saucy's voice in the outer office. I need to go wish him luck tonight. What time do you need me this afternoon?"

"My appointment is at two o'clock, so maybe around three o'clock I'll be done. I can text you."

"Okay. I will pick you up."

"Thank you, Cora. I really appreciate it."

"You're welcome. I'll see you later." Cora disconnected the call. It was silly to hold a grudge against the man for being himself. She was just fortunate that she learned about his true demeanor early enough to keep her distance. No harm was done.

"Saucy! So glad you stopped by! Are you all ready for tonight's opening night?"

"Oh, you know how I get, Mayor. My stomach is full of butterflies and tree frogs even though it's hours away yet. That first night is the hardest."

"You have been splendid at all of our town plays. You're a real local celebrity, Saucy. You have nothing to worry about. Everyone looks forward to seeing your part."

"Really?"

"Of course! When a new play is cast, my friends always ask if you have a role. They enjoy watching you. You really have a knack for acting."

"I never knew. You know, I never did volunteer in school for it. We did a few plays, and I went along if they made me, but I never thought I'd be any good. I'm not much for faking stuff, so I didn't think I could fool anybody. Eleanor has taught me a lot about immersion in a character and how to become somebody else for a little while. It's really powerful stuff!"

"Eleanor Cline has taught drama at the high school for a long time. She's probably enjoying this chance to work with adults for a change of pace."

"She great to work with."

"I know you'll make her proud tonight, Saucy. She's told me you are her best pupil!"

"I hope so, Mayor. I'll do my best!"

"I know you will." Cora Mae waved as Saucy turned to walk back out into the lobby.

"You know you do this for every play." Amanda smirked. "Mr. Salzman comes in here the first day of every play and you tell him he's great."

"He needs his confidence fluffed a little. I've had a lot of practice at that." Cora chuckled.

"Each time you do it, it's like it's the first time." Amanda shrugged.

"He is actually quite good in these plays and people do love seeing him. He just needs to push out the self-doubt. I used to do the same things with my students, the ones that were letting their confidence defeat them before a big test. If you can direct their thoughts in a positive way, they begin to believe they can be successful. Sometimes thinking it, is all it takes to make it come true. The power of positive thought is immense."

"Well, I'm going to try it on Mrs. Keslar's party and see if I can convince myself that I am worthy of attending the function. Maybe I can fool myself into having a good time!"

"We may have to work on each other to get that done." Cora Mae laughed. She was not looking forward to the event, but she couldn't bear to miss it either.

Chapter 20

"Chief?" Officer Eugene Tabor stood at Conrad's office door with his cell phone in his hand. "I've got something I need to show you."

"Okay. Come on in. What have you got there?"

"Well, I went out to Irenic Wellness and talked to Olivia D'Asaro. She's the girl that spent the night out there to keep an eye on the place."

"Oh, Peter Jessup's girlfriend!"

"Yeah. He stayed out there, too, so he was there when Wink showed up."

"You got pictures?" Conrad reached for Tabor's phone.

"Yeah, but Olivia recorded a video I wanted you to see."

Conrad's eyes widened! "Did she get the sheriff on there?"

"No, just the other guy." Tabor handed his phone to Conrad and taped the play button. Aside from a few words between Peter and Olivia, you could only hear a faint tap as the siding was ripped from the back of the building.

“She started recording when he took the crowbar to the siding. In just a second, you’ll see Wink pull in and his headlights hit the guy’s face. I don’t know him, but maybe we’ll find someone that does.”

Conrad hit the button to pause the video when Wink pulled in. “Nope.” Conrad shook his head. “I don’t recognize him. Who did the vehicle tag come back to?” Conrad handed the phone back.

“The truck is registered to the mine.”

“The mine! I didn’t see that coming.” Conrad chuckled. “I bet Kimball or Snell know him then. Show that to them. I think they’ve talked to everybody who works out there.”

“Right, Chief. I’ll ask them.”

“Where are they?”

“They just came in. I think they were over at the victim’s mother-in-law’s house. She didn’t want to come into the office, so they both went over there. Georgia warned them that Mother Jessup was a less than pleasant person and recommended that they both go together.”

Conrad nodded. “I’ve heard the same, but I’ve not met her.”

“I think it’s just routine,” Tabor said. “Some of the guys at the mine mentioned that the mother-in-law hated the victim. It was pretty well known, so they just wanted to ask where she was Sunday.”

Conrad nodded. “Did you take a report on the vandalism at Irenic?”

“No, Chief. I assumed that the Sheriff did that. I can if you want me to. I’ve got pictures of the damage.”

“Yes, go ahead and write it up. If he asks, I’ll tell

him Mrs. Keslar and Olivia called us, so we felt required to create a report. You can add it to Wink's file."

"Gotcha."

"Oh, and Tabor. When you talk to Snell, ask him about the film. I don't know why he hasn't gotten anything back on that yet. He should have had it the next day."

"Will do, Chief."

"I'm here." Detective Sam Snell waved from the hallway. "I just got back from Mother Jessup's." Sam rolled his eyes. "She's really something!"

"So I've heard!" Conrad chuckled. "I was just telling Tabor here to ask you about the film. Any word on what they found?"

Detective Snell huffed. "Still working on that. It seems the film canister is lost."

"Lost!" Conrad rocked back in his chair.

"Yeah, the guys in the evidence room checked it in, but when they went to get it for developing, the canister isn't there. They're looking for it." Sam put his hands in his pockets and shrugged his shoulders. "I'm sure somebody is in hot water for it."

"Oh, I've got a video to show you." Eugene handed Sam his cell phone and tapped the button to start the video. "It's only a couple of minutes long, but there is one really clear shot at the very end. That's the guy that Sheriff Bell picked up last night. He was vandalizing the new spa. The Chief thought you might know who he was."

Sam Snell's head came up, and he returned the phone to Officer Tabor. "That's Noah Yates. He's the blaster."

"The what?" Eugene pocketed his phone. "The

blaster?"

"Yeah. He's a new guy that Walter Slope hired when he got here. He's been blasting around the perimeter to close off some unused tunnels. He was in the office Monday. I guess you didn't see him."

"I don't think he's from around here." Conrad shook his head. "I wonder why Sheriff Bell seemed to know him. Why would he care about a mine blaster?"

"And why would a miner vandalize a new business?" Officer Tabor scratched his head. "It's not like he was trying to break into the place. He was just trying to damage it. It doesn't make sense."

"What happened last night? I must have missed something." Sam held his hands up. "Sheriff Bell was here in Spicetown?"

Conrad handed Wink's police report from the evening incident to Detective Snell. "He was out at the Irenic Wellness Spa. They've been having trouble out there and had an employee spending the night to keep an eye on things. When she saw this guy show up, he just waited until Sheriff Bell arrived. They talked a bit and then he started tearing up the place. That's when the employee called us. She took the video."

Sam's mouth was hanging open for several seconds. "Where's the guy now?

"Sheriff Bell took him." Conrad shrugged. "It was his jurisdiction. Wink couldn't do anything but write it up."

"For starters, Sheriff Bell doesn't patrol. At all. Never has." Detective Snell shook his head and stared out the window. "This doesn't make any sense. Who owns this place? Is it a rival of his?"

"No. Grace Keslar owns it, and it doesn't open

until after the first of the year. She lives just south of town, a wealthy lady in her eighties. She's never mentioned Sheriff Bell. I know when any little thing happens, she always calls us because we're closer. I can't imagine any connection between them." Conrad took a sip of coffee. "Maybe she contributed money to his opponent. Bell can be vengeful."

"I could see that," Sam Snell said. "Pay back."

"I've just never known her to be political, but then again, she can't vote in Spicetown city elections, so I might not have any way to know."

"That seems really petty." Officer Tabor shook his head and looked down at his feet.

"You're right, Tabor, but there's got to be some reason he's in the middle of this and we're just not seeing it." Conrad glanced at Sam, hoping he would find the missing piece.

§

"I'm running over to the library now and dropping off this box of extra Christmas decorations I had at home. Cece said they needed something new this year."

Amanda nodded.

"Then I'm running over to the Carom Seed Craft Corner to pick up my skirt for the party. I'm quite proud to say that I had to ask Peggy Cochran to take it in a couple of inches for me." Cora Mae posed with one hand on her hip and the other held up in the air like a vintage model.

Amanda giggled. "That's wonderful. All of that walking and eating healthy paid off."

"I just hope all of my neglect during the winter

doesn't reverse it."

"You'll get back to it once spring is here."

"Yes," Cora said. "I'm planning to do that. Peggy has done several alterations for me. I wish I could do that myself, but I only know how to hem slacks. She does the waistband for me. It will only take a second though because she said it was ready for pickup."

"Then you have a hair appointment." Amanda pointed at Cora Mae. The appointment was with Amanda's mother, so she usually kept close watch on those.

"I do! Anything I need to watch out for?" Cora smiled. Since Amanda began planning her wedding to Bryan, her mother had been trying to glean any insider information she could from Cora. "Any topic I need to avoid or angle I need to be prepared for."

"No, she's been pretty quiet lately. I've explained that I'm not having a huge wedding and she's sulked about that. Hopefully, she's adjusting to the news."

"Walter Slope called me this morning and asked if I'd pick him up from his dentist appointment this afternoon. He's getting a tooth pulled at two o'clock. He needs a ride home so I may not come back from the beauty shop. It just depends on when your mom is done with me."

"You guys are talking again." Amanda glanced at Cora out of the side of her eye.

"No, not really. He just doesn't have anybody else. I know it's hard when you're new in town and only know your own employees. He doesn't have anyone else to ask."

Amanda nodded. "So, you may not be back today. I got it."

"If the Chief needs me, you can tell him to call my

cell phone. Otherwise, I'm looking forward to getting home early today. This holiday season is wearing me out this year. Maybe I'm getting too old for all this. I'm going to put my feet up tonight and relax."

Sheri Richey

Chapter 21

Cora was relieved to find the dentist waiting room was empty. “Mayor Bingham! How nice to see you!” Nancy Hegler greeted Cora from the counter when she walked into the dentist office. Nancy had been a student of Cora’s when she was a new teacher and she had also taught Nancy’s son, James.

“Good afternoon, Nancy. I’ve come by to give Mr. Slope a ride home. He asked me to pick him up because he said he wouldn’t be able to drive after his dental procedure.”

“Mr. Slope said you would be coming by,” Nancy smiled and then covered her mouth with her hand. Leaning forward she whispered, “We didn’t believe him though.” Nancy’s laughter was infectious, and Cora found herself relaxing from the tension this outing had created.

“I’m trying to help our newcomer. He doesn’t really know anyone in town except his employees and you can’t really ask them for this kind of help.”

“Certainly not! I know you are trying to do the

neighborly thing. I'll warn you though, he's taken to that anesthesia a little better than some do." Nancy giggled. "He's a little giddy."

"Oh, my." Cora frowned. She expected this to be awkward, but this sounded as though it could be even more than that.

"Don't worry. Dr. Kagel is going to come out with him and help him to your car."

"Dr. Kagel?" Cora had recommended Dr. Brasley.

"Yes, Dr. Kagel is here on an internship. He'll be right out."

Cora nodded and took a seat in the lobby. Soon she began to hear singing.

"God rest ye merry gentlemen, let nothing you dismay." Fairly certain it was Walter's voice, Cora Mae chuckled. He did have a nice baritone sound. Perhaps the comedy of the situation would absolve the discomfort.

The door to the inner office opened forcefully and Walter came out singing with his arm looped in the arm of a young man wearing white.

"Are you here to pick up Mr. Slope?"

"Yes, I am." Cora smiled.

"I'm Dr. Kagel. I'll help him down to your car if you'll show me where you're parked."

"Away in a manager, no—. Cora! Thank you so much for coming."

Cora nodded to Nancy and waved goodbye. "You're welcome. Now, where on Tarragon Street do you live, Walter?"

"Right by the tanning salon. I'll show you." Walter waved for Cora to follow. "Silent Night. Holy Night."

"Mr. Slope, you need to hold onto that railing

while we go down these few stairs." Dr. Kagel waited for Walter to grab the rail before slowly taking his first step. There were only five short steps to the lobby of the office building. "Concentrate, Mr. Slope. We don't want you to fall."

"Oh, I'm okay. Five golden rings! Four calling birds--"

"Walter, maybe you should stop singing now. You might be disturbing the other businesses."

"Oh! Right. Right, Cora. Sorry. I was just practicing for the play. I feel pretty good so far. Maybe I can perform tonight."

"No, Mr. Slope. I don't think that's a good idea," Dr. Kagel said as he glanced over his shoulder at Cora Mae. "Pretty soon the shot is going to wear off and you will probably want to take some pain medication. That should make you pretty sleepy. I don't think you should plan on doing anything this evening."

"Oh, I already took one of those! I don't feel sleepy at all."

Once they reached the bottom of the steps, Cora ran around them to open the door to the street. "There's my car. Right there. Let me open the door."

Cora opened the passenger side door and stood back for Dr. Kagel to drop Walter in the seat. Walter's singing was beginning to slur, and he sounded as though the wind was coming out of his sails slightly. "Walter, do you need to stop anywhere before I drop you off at home?"

"Oh, I think you ought to go straight home, ma'am." Dr. Kagel pushed Walter's knee inside the car and slammed the door. "If he's taken a pain pill, he'll need to sleep."

"Oh, dear." Cora ran around the car. "Thank you,

doctor. I'll get him straight home."

Cora waved as she pulled away from the curb and sensed Walter's quiet decline. "Tell me, Walter. Did you like the doctor? Did everything go well?"

"Yes," Walter said, nodding his head slowly. "That is Dr. Bryce. He was nice." Walter snorted. "That rhymes! Just like mice." His words were flowing slowly and slightly slurred.

"Walter, that was Dr. Kagel."

"Kagel Bryce!" Walter stabbed at the air. "No, Bryce Kagel. Nice young man."

Cora turned down Clove Street for the short two block drive. "Your apartment is next to the Safflower Tanning Salon?" Cora glanced over and Walter's chin was resting on his chest. She elbowed him a couple of times. "Walter! Don't go to sleep yet."

"Yalp. Yep, that's right."

"Next to the tanning salon?"

"Up! Up, up and away!"

"What's the address, Walter?"

"It's 326B." Walter pointed as they approached the tanning salon and Cora pulled over to the curb.

Cora looked in the window of the salon and saw the number 326 over the doorway. "That's the address of the salon." Parking the car, Cora looked over and Walter's chin was down again. "Walter! That's the salon. Where is your place?""

Walter moaned and furrowed his brow. "Up." He sighed heavily and tried to point. "Up above."

"Oh, no? Do we have to go upstairs? Or is there an elevator? Where is the door? Walter? Walter!" Cora grabbed his arm and shook him, but the best she could get him to emit was a groan. "Oh, Walter! Don't do this to me." Staring at him slumped against the window, she saw he began to drool, and she opened her own car door to jump out.

Peering through the window of the tanning salon, no one was at the register, but she looked a few doors down and saw a blue door with 326 above it. When she pushed it open, there was a flight of stairs and several doors at the top of the steps. Pulling out her cellphone, she called Conrad's cell phone.

"Connie, I hate to bother you, but is Eugene free? I need some help."

"Sure. He's here in the office."

"I picked up Walter Slope from the dentist because he couldn't drive home after a dental procedure, but now he's fallen asleep in my car. I need to get him up some stairs over the Safflower Tanning Salon. Do you think Eugene could help him up there?"

"He's asleep?"

"He took some pain medication, and he should have waited until he got home. I had planned to just drop him off, but it's turned into a bigger problem than that. I'm out in front of the Salon on Tarragon Street."

"Are you sure he doesn't need medical attention?" Conrad stifled a chuckle.

Cora looked at Walter through the windshield as his chest rose and fell. "He's breathing fine. I just can't get him to stand up and walk."

"Okay. We'll be right over."

"Thank you." Cora closed her eyes and took a calming breath. Conrad was probably having a good laugh over this.

§

"This is my dear girl, Olive." Grace Keslar waved her arm toward Olive. "Olive dear, this is Dorothy Parish, owner of the Caraway Cafe. Have you met?"

"No, Miss Trawl." Olive curtsied stiffly and glanced up at Dorothy from a bowed head seemingly timid in Grace's presence.

"Hi, Olive." Dorothy smiled. "Mrs. Keslar, I'd like to bring some supplies in from my car. Imogene said she could store them for me for this weekend. If it's okay, I'll pull around back."

"Whatever you need, Dorothy. Please coordinate with Olive. She will assist you." Grace wandered away as if distracted by a sound no one else heard.

"I'll just pull around to the back by the garden. Is that okay?" Dorothy looked at Olive curiously. "Are you okay?"

"Yes. Yes, I'm okay. I'll meet you at the back door and help you carry."

"That would be great. I appreciate it." Dorothy returned to her car and pulled around a gravel drive slowly snaking behind the mansion, past the gardens and a sitting area with covered lawn furniture through a carriage house to a back door with a large, bricked deck. Olive stood waiting for her as she slowed to a stop.

Dorothy opened the back of her van. "If you could grab one of those boxes, I'll get these platters."

Olive picked up the box and led Dorothy in through the kitchen door. "Imogene, where should we put these?"

"Hello, Ms. Dorothy! What do you have here? Oh, the box definitely needs to go into the walk-in."

Imogene pointed to direct Olive to the large walk-in refrigerated storage area. "There is plenty of room in there."

"Thank you, Imogene," Dorothy called out as she walked by and then returned for another trip to her van. "Have you been able to find enough servers for the party? Frank told me there is a service in Paxton that he's heard good things about. If you need the phone number, I can get it for you."

"Thank you, but right now I think I've got enough. Mrs. Keslar said she got help from the young woman that works at her spa. I don't know if they used a service or not, but she says the issue is being handled."

"I'm glad it worked out." Dorothy turned to make another trip outside with Olive close on her heels. "I think that may be all, if you can take this last tray inside."

"I can take that." Olive held out her arms. "Have you been out to the new spa?"

"No, I haven't," Dorothy said as she reached for the van door. "Have you?"

"Not yet, but I'm hoping I get a sneak peek after the party. I'm not sure when it's going to open, but it sounds like it's a beautiful place."

"Maybe Mrs. Keslar will have a grand opening out there soon." Dorothy said as she slammed the doors shut. She wasn't sure she wanted to cater that one. This had been exhausting. "Thanks for all of your help, Olive."

"It's Rosa. Oh, never mind. You're welcome." Olive waved goodbye as Dorothy pulled away.

Sheri Richey

Chapter 22

"Thanks, Tabor. See you tomorrow." Conrad slapped Officer Tabor on the back as he left Walter Slope's apartment. "I'll get a ride back with the mayor."

"Yes, thank you, Eugene," Cora called out from her seat on Walter's sofa. "I appreciate your help."

"You're welcome. Have a good evening."

Cora studied Conrad as they listened to Tabor's footsteps descend the stairs. "I guess he will be okay." Cora frowned. "Do you think it's all right to leave him?"

Glancing into Walter's bedroom, Conrad scowled. "Well, he's sleeping." Conrad and Eugene had basically been forced to drag Walter up the stairs and once Cora wrenched his apartment keys from his coat pocket, they tossed him on his bed. He was sleeping soundly.

"It smells like cinnamon in here." Conrad frowned.

"Yes, he chews on those cinnamon toothpicks all

the time." Cora sniffed. "He makes them himself."

"He sure reacted heavily to the medication. I'm a little concerned that might have happened because it conflicts with another medication he takes."

Cora stood up. "Let me look in the medicine cabinet. I hate to snoop, but you may be right, and it could be dangerous to leave him unattended."

Conrad paced the living room while Cora Mae tinkered in the medicine cabinet and linen closet. Walking out of the bathroom, she held up a prescription bottle. "He has a prescription for an anti-anxiety medicine. That may be what he took."

"That probably shouldn't have been added at the same time. I wonder if he even disclosed it to the dentist. People are always reluctant to tell others about anti-anxiety meds."

"That might explain the deep sleep, but I wouldn't think it would be dangerous. I'm going to give the dentist's office a call and tell them what we're dealing with here. Hopefully, they can offer some guidance." Cora pulled her phone from her handbag and searched in her contacts for the dentist.

Conrad ambled around the living room, checked out the window then reached for a small, framed photo propped on a table near the door.

"No one is answering. I guess Walter was the last patient for the day and they've gone home." Cora tossed the phone back in her purse and pursed her lips. "I don't know anyone to call for him. I don't think it's appropriate for me to hold a vigil at his house. I had only planned to drive up to the curb and drop him off. I just wish I knew someone to tell about his condition. Do you know anyone in the mine office? Maybe an assistant or something?"

"I think I found someone." Conrad carried the framed photo over to Cora. "This guy."

Cora took the photo from Conrad's hand and then Conrad tapped on the face of a young man who had his arm around a slightly younger Walter. Below the photo, a banner read 'Happy Father's Day 2015'

"Walter has a son?" Cora looked up at Conrad. "He never mentioned anything about it to me."

"That young man is working out at the mine right now."

Cora handed the photo back to Conrad. "Why didn't he say something? Why didn't he pick up his dad at the dentist? Who is he?"

Conrad returned the framed photo to the hall table. "Let's go back to the station. I know Detective Snell has interviewed him, so he'll have contact information for him. We'll let the son take care of his dad. Then we can get some dinner."

"A good plan!" Cora turned her ear to the doorway and heard Walter's heavy breathing. Nodding, she followed Conrad down the stairs.

§

"Why did you pick this place?" Peter Jessup looked up at the church entrance and then started to walk around the truck.

"Come back here." Noah Yates leaned out of his truck window and waved his hand motioning for Peter to come back.

"I'm getting in! It's cold out here." The wind whistled around his collar and the temperature had dropped when the sun went down.

"No, you're not. This isn't going to take long."

Noah growled and slapped a small stack of bills in his hand.

“Why did you pick this place? They’ve probably got cameras.” Peter pointed at the building. Another reason to get inside the truck. He didn’t like being exposed outside.

“It’s a church! Nobody patrols a church.” Noah rolled his eyes. “Here’s your money.”

Pulling his hand back when Peter reached for it, Noah frowned. “Wait. What’s up with that girl over there.” Noah pointed to the Irenic Wellness Center across the road. “Is she crazy? She almost got me arrested!”

“Almost! I saw you get arrested. I was in there, too. What happened?”

“Nothing.” Noah shrugged.

“Didn’t you see our cars out front? What in the world were you doing anyway?”

“Did you call the cops?”

“No, I didn’t, but my girlfriend did. That’s the whole reason we were out there.”

“You were staking it out?” Noah shouted.

“We were supposed to keep an eye on the place and then you come up. Our cars were right out front! Why would you stop?”

“Yeah, but I didn’t see any lights on. I thought somebody just left the cars. I looked around. What were you doing in the dark?” Noah tossed his head back and laughed. “Oh, I get it. She was on building patrol, and you were on the prowl.”

Peter shook his head and rolled his eyes. “The back windows are all tinted. The only place that you can see lights are at the entrance of the building, so we didn’t turn those on.”

Noah shrugged. “No big deal, I guess. No harm done, but you should have stopped her. It was almost a big mess. I don’t know why she had to call the Spicetown cops. The Sheriff was already there, and this place isn’t even in Spicetown.”

“That’s what the owner told her to do. Why was the Sheriff there? And he didn’t do anything?”

“Nah, he just waited for everybody to leave and brought me back to my truck.”

“You took a crowbar to the building!” Peter shrieked.

“Forget about it. Here’s your money. Are you interested in more?”

Peter took the bills and counted them. “Maybe.” Pocketing the bills, he left his hands in his pockets. “Depends.”

“Tomorrow after five o’clock—“

“I can’t do tomorrow,” Peter stepped back. “My wife’s funeral is at two.”

“It’ll be done by five!”

“But my mom is having people over.” Peter shook his head and stared down at his feet while he kicked the small gravel around. “I can’t do that. Maybe later. After seven. I could probably get free then. Can’t it wait until seven?”

“Yeah, I guess so. I’ll meet you there at seven. Same spot. Don’t bring the girlfriend!” Noah tossed his head back laughing as he put the truck in reverse and pulled out of the parking spot.

Peter nodded and rushed around to get inside his own car. Starting the engine, he flipped the vents open and turned the heat to full blast. His hands and feet were numb from the cold. As he reached to put the car in reverse, he saw car lights across the street.

A white sedan pulled out of the Irenic Wellness Center parking lot onto the road and turned toward Spicetown, following Noah. Peter hadn't noticed a car parked over there when he had pulled in the church. Maybe it had pulled in while they were talking.

A private security company patrolling the building for the owner, perhaps? He would need to ask Olivia about it when he saw her later tonight.

§

"Hey, Sam. It's Chief Harris." Conrad's office chair squeaked when he rocked back in it.

"Hey Chief."

"I just got back in the office and the dispatcher, Officer Crawford, told me you left a little while ago."

"Yeah, about half an hour ago."

"Well, I wanted to know if you have contact information on Noah Yates. I have a situation here and I think I need to talk to him."

"Yeah, I've got his phone number. He and another guy have an apartment in Paxton."

"It sounds like you're driving."

"I'm in the car. Gwen and I were just going to get something to eat."

"Oh, okay. Well, it appears that Noah Yates is the son of Walter Slope."

"What?!" Sam touched his foot to his brake pedal to slow his speed, so his mind could process the information that Conrad had just shared.

"How did you find this out, Chief?" Gwen Kimball squirmed in her seat and glanced at Sam.

"I had to help Walter into his apartment this

afternoon. Long crazy story, but I saw a photo on the table in his place. It was dated 2015, but it was Walter and Noah, arms around each other and a caption that said Happy Father's Day."

"Wow!" Sam struggled to focus on the drive and the new information at the same time.

"Kind of makes sense though," Gwen said as she pointed at a side road, directing Sam to pull the car in and turn around.

"I guess that's how Noah got his job." Conrad chuckled.

"We've learned that Noah has some job troubles of his own. It explains why Walter would hire him." Sam nodded as he pulled into a parking place. "He's had some accidents at other mines and been suspended by the State. I'm sure he can't get a job easily."

"Ah, that does make sense then," Conrad said.

"Did you want to talk to Noah about Walter?"

"Yeah, but only to tell him his dad might need a welfare check tonight. Walter had a dental procedure today and the pain medicine hit him pretty hard. I thought I'd encourage Noah to check on him, but I won't do that if you'd rather not tip your hand on this." Conrad waited but did not receive a response. "Maybe you know of another miner that I could call instead. Does Walter have an assistant or someone who might check on him. He's at his apartment here in Spicetown and he was sleeping when I left. Maybe he'll be okay. I just—"

"You know, Chief. I just happen to know where Noah is right now. I'll let him know. Maybe I can tip him off to check on Walter without telling him we know about his family connection."

Conrad hummed. "Sounds good to me. I'm headed out for dinner, too. I'll leave it with you then. See you tomorrow."

Chapter 23

"Good morning, Chief." Sam Snell walked in the side door, the employee's entrance of the Spicetown Police Department, as if he worked there. He'd spent every day there that week and the staff had finally adopted him.

"Hey, Sam. Did you catch up with Noah Yates last night?"

"I did." Sam grinned and Conrad motioned him towards the chair in his office. "When you called, it just so happened that Gwen and I were following him. He met with Peter Jessup in the church parking lot across from the Irenic Wellness Center last night. Gwen and I were across the street watching them."

Conrad's eyes opened wide. "Peter and Noah? At church?"

Sam chuckled. "It's possible they know each other from work, but Noah hasn't been there long. He came when Walter was transferred. They can't know each other well."

"But to meet in an empty lot, they must be up to

something."

Sam scratched his chin. "I think there was a pay off, but I can't say for certain. Peter was standing outside the truck and Noah handed him something. I couldn't see what it was."

"Noah paid Peter? When you said payoff, I expected it to be the other way around. Were you watching them because you think Peter is involved in Jane's death?" Conrad took a sip of coffee and pointed at the pot as an offering to Sam.

Sam shook his head. "It was all an accident, really. Gwen and I left here planning to go to dinner. I suggested we drive out to Irenic for a second because I wanted to see the damage on the back of the building after seeing the video Officer Tabor showed us. While we were driving around the building, this whole thing happened across the street. I just parked so we could watch. They weren't paying attention at all."

"Must mean they weren't worried about being seen. I'm sure the church has cameras on the parking lot or at least at the front door." Conrad tapped his hand on his desk. "It's an odd spot to meet though unless they were going different directions. Did they turn opposite ways when they left?"

"I followed Noah. He left first and headed to Spicetown. That's when you called. Peter was just sitting in the church lot, and I didn't see him leave." Sam scrolled through his phone.

"Peter lives east of town. I can't imagine he would pull out north on that road anyway."

"I don't know," Sam said, tapping on his phone screen. "But I got the autopsy results back this morning."

"It's about time!"

"I know it's been slow moving, but everybody takes off around the holidays. It's hard to get information."

"What did the autopsy show? Any surprises?"

"Head trauma, which we already knew, but the particles were interesting. They thought she'd been shot at first. It was a small round entry wound on the surface."

"I saw it when her body was found." Conrad nodded. "But it was on the top of her head."

"Yeah, but it wasn't a bullet that made that wound." Sam sat back in his chair. "It was a rock."

"A rock?" Conrad furrowed his brow and gazed out the window.

"They sent a picture of it. It's not very big." Sam handed his cell phone to Conrad. "There were actually smaller entry wounds on her as well, but the one we saw on top of her head was the cause of death. It penetrated her skull."

"Flyrock." Conrad gasped. "Oh, no. When this gets out, the community is going to be in an uproar."

"What's that mean? Flyrock?" Sam leaned forward on his knees.

"Flyrock is the projectile, the fragment of rock that breaks away when the coal mines do blasting." Conrad dropped his head. "The community lives in fear of it. That subdivision out by the mine that everyone calls Miner's Meadow, it was built within the flyrock zone. The mayor told me that nobody other than miners would ever buy out there, because it was too close to the blasting, but as far as I know, there haven't been fatalities here from it. There have been fatalities in other areas though."

"Wow," Sam took a deep breath. "I expect the Sheriff to call me back to Paxton once he sees the autopsy results. No crime here."

"Maybe not a premeditated murder, but a crime, nonetheless. She was killed on Sunday and the mine had not posted any notice of the blasting. I know that, because people in the area complained about it, so the mayor checked into it. She told me that there was no approved blasting that day."

"What did she do about it?"

"Walter Slope was giving her the runaround when she inquired, so she sent a formal inquiry to the corporate office for response. She has more information on it. She knows the approximate location of the detonation."

"The dynamite couldn't have been in those woods though." Sam stood up and stretched his legs.

"They don't actually use dynamite anymore, but it's still an explosive, and that flyrock can travel well over a thousand feet. We need to get the mayor's data. I'm going by there later and I'll get you a copy of her file."

"Great. If nothing else, I know I've got to report this to the Department of Natural Resources." Sam walked toward the office door and checked his watch.

"Any luck with the film yet?" Conrad held his hands out with his palms up.

"Not yet, but they're going through the evidence room to see if it was misfiled. This happens sometimes. It may just be in the wrong box. Everybody is short staffed at the holidays."

"I know. Happens every year." Conrad shook his head.

"If Sheriff Bell doesn't pull me back to Paxton today, I'm going to check out the funeral this afternoon. I still feel like Bell is tied into this somewhere and I want to see if he shows up."

"Well, I guess I'll see you Saturday night at the mansion?" Conrad chuckled. "Kimball said she was dragging you there."

Sam laughed. "I'm actually looking forward to it. I'd like to meet Mrs. Keslar. She sounds interesting, and I'd love to see the inside of her house. I've driven by it and it's massive."

"These things aren't my cup of tea, but appearances are part of the job. You never know what will happen." Conrad smiled.

"See you later, Chief."

§

"Walter? Are you feeling better today?" Cora had not worried about Walter but had wondered throughout the evening whether he was safe. She knew Conrad had gotten word to his son to check on him, but she did not want to share her involvement in any of that.

"Good morning, Cora. Yes, I am feeling well today. I plan to participate in the play tonight and I expect everything will be fine."

"I'm so glad to hear that. I was a little concerned about your state yesterday..."

"Yes, well I think the medication was a little strong for me. I'm not accustomed to taking medication, and I misunderstood the directions that were given to me at the dentist office. In my defense, they gave me the instruction after I was under the influence of the sedative used during the extraction." Walter chuckled. "It was not a clear thinking time for me."

"I imagine not!"

"Then once I was up, I thought I understood their expectation was for me to take the pain medication before the other influence wore off. I didn't see any harm since I wasn't driving. I had no idea it would be so incapacitating!"

"But are you in pain today at all?"

"No, I'm a little afraid to eat, but no discomfort. I don't plan on taking any more of the medication."

"That's probably the safest solution."

"I appreciate your concern. Did you attend the play last night?"

"No, I didn't, but a few of my staff attended and they said it went very well. They enjoyed the presentation. I'm waiting to see if Saucy stops in today to give me his perceptions. He is generally quite nervous the first night, and it is a bit of a challenge getting him started. Once the opening night is over, I think he truly enjoys himself."

"I wish I could have been there to support him. I may give him a call this morning, too."

"I'm sure he would like that." Cora waved Amanda in the doorway when she peeked around the corner. "Well, –"

"Are you planning to attend the funeral today, Cora? I feel as though I should since it was the spouse of one of our employees, although I don't know Peter well."

"No, I'm not going to attend. I didn't know Jane or Peter, but my assistant Amanda will be there with her fiancé. Peter grew up in the community so I expect there will be a large turnout. You and Peter have had some challenges I believe you mentioned to me before."

"Yes, that's true. He was resistant to me when I

first arrived, and we had some disagreements. Nothing personal though. I'm sure he's grieving."

"Yes." Cora knew about the unfortunate state of their marriage, but hoped the young woman had someone who grieved for her. "Well, I should get back to work and perhaps you should get some rest this morning. Good luck this evening."

"Thank you, Cora. Have a good day."

Cora hung up the phone and blew air out through pursed lips. "Walter sounds like normal. I guess that horrible thing is over." Cora Mae had shared her disaster from the previous day with Amanda this morning and they were both in tears of laughter. It had not been funny yesterday.

"Shew!" Amanda chuckled. "At least you can shut that door now. No regrets."

"None. My responsibility has been met and yes, I'm glad that's over. The call was a bit awkward though."

Amanda nodded in agreement. "Bryan is going to pick me up at 1:30 this afternoon and Laura is going to cover for me since I won't be back today. She'll answer your phone and close for you. Bryan wants to go over to Peter's mother's house after the service."

"That's fine. Are you ready for the party tomorrow? Did you finally figure out what you are going to wear?"

"I'm as ready as I can be. For some reason, I'm a little nervous. We're going with my parents. They both know Mrs. Keslar so I'll hide behind them." Amanda shivered. "I'll try to stay off her radar. My dad says she's really nice. She just gives me a weird vibe."

"She's different." Cora smiled. "She's an animal lover though."

"Yeah, my dad says she has a cat that she thinks is

her late husband."

"What?" Cora's eyebrows pulled together in a line. "She thinks the cat is Chancellor?"

"Yeah, like reincarnation or something." Amanda shrugged. "She named him Chauncey, but she thinks he has her husband's soul or something. My dad said he is an unusual cat personality. He understands why she thinks that. He joked about how he had a long talk with the cat when he came in last time." Amanda laughed. "My dad is a nut."

Cora giggled. "How delightful. Maybe we'll get to meet Mr. Chauncey at the party."

"Who knows? He may be wearing a tuxedo with a kitty top hat!"

Both were laughing when Harvey "Saucy" Salzman stuck his head in the doorway. "You ladies have so much fun at work! Makes me wish I hadn't retired." Saucy chuckled from their infectious laughter.

"How are you, Saucy?" Cora said. "I was hoping you would stop in and give us an update on the play. How did everything go last night?"

"Oh, we had a rocky start!" Saucy held both hands up and open in amazement. "I wasn't the only one panicking this time. I thought Eleanor was going to collapse." Eleanor Cline was the high school drama teacher and the community play director for every production so far.

"Whatever for?" Cora Mae stood from her desk chair.

"Walter Slope didn't show up and nobody could find him anywhere," Saucy exclaimed dramatically using both arms waving in the air.

Cora Mae looked at Amanda. "Walter didn't plan to attend. He didn't tell you? He had a tooth pulled yesterday, and he wasn't able to come."

"No! He didn't tell anybody, and no one has been able to reach him." Saucy glanced from Amanda to Cora. "You both knew?"

"Well, yes," Cora said guiltily. "He called me yesterday and asked if I could pick him up at the dentist because they didn't want him to drive. They'd given him pain medication..."

"Oh my! I can't believe he didn't tell Eleanor. We could have had his understudy ready to go on." Saucy grabbed his head with both hands. "Unbelievable!"

"He told me he wasn't going on as if it was already decided. I never would have guessed he hadn't told Eleanor. That doesn't make sense." Cora frowned. "What did you do?"

"Eleanor tried to reach his understudy, but on last minute notice, she couldn't find him. We had to cut his part and rework the script."

"Oh, no. I'm sure you were all in a panic. Did everyone adapt smoothly? I just talked to him a few minutes ago. I called to check on how he was feeling, and he said he planned to attend tonight."

"Well, thank goodness for that. Eleanor may come apart at the seams when she sees him. I wouldn't want to be him!" Saucy chuckled. "She's probably not over it yet. Walter does have a beautiful voice though. He was missed."

"Given his unreliability, perhaps she should keep his understudy in the wings every night!"

"Good suggestion, Mayor! Have a good day!"

Sheri Richey

Chapter 24

"You should have joined me at the Caraway Cafe for lunch today, Cora." Conrad patted his bulbous stomach. "The Salisbury steak was divine! You know Frank doesn't go all out very often. You shouldn't have missed it! He must have the Christmas spirit."

Cora smiled. "I couldn't get away from the board. They scheduled an eleven o'clock meeting today, and I knew they were going to keep me late. We all get to gabbing and lose track of time."

"Hopefully you were just chatting it up and not arguing." Conrad tried to grab his ankle to keep it on his knee, but finally gave up and let it fall.

"Too close to Christmas for that. Several of them went to the Christmas play last night, and it sounds like it's really delightful. I'm looking forward to it. I think we'll like it."

"Is that Sunday?" Conrad scowled.

"Yes, we have tickets for the matinée and that's the last showing, so it should be the best. Saucy was in here today telling me that Walter didn't tell anyone he wasn't coming last night so they had a real mess right before the curtain went up."

"Why would he do that? That's inconsiderate. Did they manage okay?"

"Saucy said they had to rewrite things to work around him. I'm sure Eleanor wants to strangle him." Cora Mae grimaced. "I can't believe Christmas is next week. I feel like it just flew up on me and I didn't do any of the preparations I usually do."

"You have things on auto-pilot now. The decorations for the city are all planned, you have the Turners doing the trees, you have the community center events all scheduled way ahead of time. You can just sit back and relax now. Let the holiday season happen." Conrad chuckled.

"I suppose," Cora Mae said wistfully. She was so efficient she had become unnecessary. "I still have Christmas dinner to cook. It may be just us this year. You know your buddy, Ned, is going skiing, so he won't be joining us."

"Yeah, I'd like to see that!" Conrad snorted.

"Violet stayed in Arizona with her daughter this year and Saucy said he was going over to his sister's house. I invited Amanda and Bryan, but I didn't expect them to come. They are going to her family's house. Next year, she may be the one making the Christmas dinner!"

"Yeah, I guess she'll be Mrs. Stotlar by that time." Conrad tapped his foot.

"Oh, I did invite Walter Slope originally, but I'm hoping he's forgotten about it. It will be awkward, if he comes. Things are a little tense between us now."

Conrad's eyebrows went up. "Are they?"

"Yes, I've seen a side to him that I wasn't very fond

of, so I've distanced myself from that friendship."

Conrad hummed.

"I felt sorry for him being away from family and friends, working in a new area at this time of the year, but now that I know he has a son here, I'm hoping the two of them can do something special together for the holidays."

"Well, the reason I stopped in was to share some news that isn't going to make you happy, but you need to know."

Cora dropped her head down dramatically. "Can it wait until next year?"

Conrad chuckled. "I know you don't like surprises."

Cora Mae straightened up. "You're right. I don't. What's going on?"

"Sam got the autopsy results back today on Jane."

Cora Mae nodded. "Did it have surprises in it? I thought she was struck on the head, maybe from a fall."

"No," Conrad said, shaking his foot back and forth at the ankle. "In fact, they first thought she might have been shot. The wound was small and in an odd place on the top of her head."

"Oh, no." Cora Mae cupped her cheeks with her hands. "Is it flyrock? I know they were blasting the day she was reported missing. I had this sick feeling that the two situations were linked."

Conrad nodded.

"Her death was caused by the mine!" Cora slapped her hands on her desk. "This is just what everyone has worried about since the blasting started up again. Walter is going to have to answer for this!"

"And his son," Conrad added. "He's the one doing

the blasting."

"Oh, my. Has Sam reported it to the State yet?"

"I don't know if he reached them yet. He's at the funeral now. Sam asked if he could get copies of your notice and the maps. I told him you had done some research on the reports from that Sunday. They will help with his report."

"Of course! I'm happy to supply what I have."

"Is that why you started gathering the information? Did you think the two were connected from the beginning?" Conrad narrowed his eyes.

"I hoped it was not the cause, but I wanted to be prepared if it was. I don't want to see the mine close. It's a source of revenue for the county and a livelihood for our citizens, but it's deadly when they are blasting without proper controls. I don't like to see people living in fear. We have to get some peace of mind that all efforts are being made to do this responsibly..."

Conrad smiled.

"I know." Cora threw her hands up in the air. "You've heard this speech a million times."

Conrad laughed as his phone pinged with a text message.

"I'm sorry. I get carried away," Cora said sheepishly.

Conrad scowled at his phone display. "We've got trouble at the funeral." Moaning as he rose from his chair, he hitched his belt up and grabbed his coat. "I guess I need to get out there. Georgia sent Tabor out, but he might need help."

"What kind of trouble? How do you get in trouble at a funeral!?" Cora stood up just as her phone chimed. Amanda sent a message that Peter and Trevor were brawling while Mother Jessup was screaming at them both. “Oh, my.” Cora shook her head. “Both boys and his mom?”

Conrad hesitated. “Peter’s mom is in it, too?”

“Amanda’s text says the boys are fighting and Peter’s mom is screaming at them both.”

“I’ll call you later.” Conrad growled and muttered under his breath as he shuffled out of Cora’s office door. Cora texted Amanda that the Chief was on his way.

§

"Did you see what happened here?” Conrad almost didn’t recognize Officer Kimball in plain clothes at first glance. She was off work and had decided to attend the funeral with Detective Snell.

“Couldn’t miss it.” Gwen smiled. “Peter was giving the eulogy and Trevor made some disruptive remarks during the delivery. Peter finished, but then when Trevor got up to speak, Peter told him he had no right. Everything went south from that point on.”

“Who took the first swing?” Conrad tilted his chin down.

“Peter, but Trevor created the situation with his inappropriate remarks.” Gwen shook her head. “He lit the match, so to speak.”

Conrad shrugged. Not an uncommon situation to see both sides fueling the fire, but trash talk wasn’t illegal. “Anybody pressing charges?”

“Of course!” Sam Snell said as he approached. “Everybody thinks they want to. I told them to go down to the station and whoever got there first, could file a report.”

Conrad laughed. “Have they both run off now?”

"Yep! They both took off, so no transport needed after all. They can drive themselves down there. Hopefully, there won't be an accident from them trying to race each other!" Sam swiped his palms together.

"What about Mother Jessup?" Conrad looked around, but he didn't see Peter's mother in the crowd.

"She made more noise than the boys. She disappeared as well, so I'm assuming she took Peter to the station, or she went down there to referee." Sam looked around and shook his head. "Glad I'm not going back there."

Conrad chuckled. "I may stick around here and manage crowd control myself. The PD may not be the best place to be right now. I should probably at least warn Georgia about what's coming."

"I'll give her a call," Gwen said, pulling her cell phone from her coat pocket.

"I'm a little surprised that I don't see many miners here," Conrad said. "I know you said Peter wasn't very popular, but I always think people will pull together when the worst happens. I would have expected them to show for his wife. From what I could tell, no one had anything bad to say about her."

Sam nodded. "I think a lot of the spouses are here, those that lived near Jane and Peter in Miner's Meadow. I recognize some faces. Maybe they couldn't get off work. I was surprised Walter Slope wasn't here."

Conrad watched the groups of people dissolve and move out the front door of the funeral home. "Yeah, I'm surprised, too. Then again, maybe the mine wants to distance itself from the situation. Did you file your report with the State yet?"

"No, I turned in my report and I'm waiting for the go ahead." Sam slipped his arm in his coat. "Peter doesn't know either. I haven't told the family about the autopsy results yet. I wasn't sure where everything stood. Jane's aunt was here today. She traveled down from Pennsylvania for the funeral."

"Yeah, Peter told me originally that Jane had no family at all, but that's not true," Gwen said when she rejoined them.

"Peter's still next of kin though, despite the situation." Sam buttoned his coat and helped Gwen on with hers.

"Oh, I talked to Georgia, but she said nobody has shown up at the station yet." Gwen shrugged her shoulders. "They've had plenty of time to get there. They must have gotten lost."

Sam huffed. "They probably both ran off in different directions."

Conrad waved to the couple as they got into Sam's car and backed out. As he walked to his own car, he saw a truck pull out of a parking place in the back of the lot and the driver sure looked like Noah Yates. Maybe blaster's remorse had gotten the better of him.

Sheri Richey

Chapter 25

"Are you Olive?" Jill Seabrook hollered through the locked glass doors of the Irenic Wellness Center on Saturday morning. Grace Keslar had left a voice mail on the business phone saying she was sending an employee named Olive out to Irenic with a package.

"That's me!" Olive waved one hand while clutching a box with the other and bouncing on her toes for warmth. A large bag hung from her shoulder and a fur-edged hood bobbed on her head. The morning was chilly, and the wind was high. She was anxious to get inside where it was warm.

"Hi," Jill said as she pulled the door open to Olive. "Come on inside."

"Thank you! It's cold out there today." Olive pushed her hood back and hugged the box in front of her.

"Mrs. Keslar said you were bringing us something? Is that it?" Jill pointed to the box.

"Yes. It came to the house by mistake. She

ordered it for the spa and I guess accidentally put her home address on it. She wanted you to have it. I have no idea what it is." Olive shrugged.

"Come on in. You can leave it on the table in here." Jill led her into a meeting room adjacent to her office.

"I begged and begged her all morning to let me bring it out to you. I'm dying to see the place, just dying. She talks about it all the time and I'm so interested. I hope I can join as soon as you open. Do you think Mrs. K would give me a discount since I'm an employee?"

Jill chuckled. "I couldn't say, but would you like a tour?"

"Oh, I was hoping you'd offer. I hated to ask, but yes! Yes, I'd love to see the different rooms. I want to see the yoga room. She told me about the mats in there, and the room where spin class is going to be. She said the bikes are here now and you put them together." Olive slid the box on the table and followed Jill.

"I did with help from my assistant. Let's start over here." Jill directed Olive to the yoga class rooms, and they walked through them. "These two rooms have a retractable wall, so we can make it one large area if we need to. Right now, we plan to hold two separate classes in the evening, but it's nice to have options."

"I love all the colors," Olive said pointing to the geometric shapes on the walls.

"Those represent the seven chakras. The meditation room is next door."

"This is beautiful," Olive whispered. "It's so peaceful."

"That's the goal!" Jill smiled. "The weight room

will be here." They both peeked in the door. "Not much here yet. The equipment hasn't arrived."

Nodding, Olive pointed at the door to the next room. "This must be spin class."

"Yes. Have you done it before?"

"I have once, and I loved it. I can't wait!" Olive hugged herself and bounced on the balls of her feet.

"Well, we may be hiring trainers next year to teach classes so that might be something you would enjoy."

"Oh, I would. I would love that." Walking back toward the office, Olive glanced around the center waiting room. "You have an assistant?"

"I do, but she's not working today."

"Well, Mrs. Keslar told me to tell you to lock up the place at noon and take the afternoon off, so you can get ready for the party. She's expecting you at her Christmas party tonight."

"I'll be there!" Jill smiled. "What do you do for Mrs. Keslar now? Do you work at her house?"

"I do, but there's been a bunch of extra stuff to do because of the party. On top of that, she wants the house ready for any overnight guests that want to visit the spa, so we are opening a lot of the rooms that were pretty much sealed up before. Have you seen her house?"

"Only from the outside."

"Oh! You've got to come early then, and I'll show you around. It's magnificent! She has twenty-six bedrooms. We've only got nine of them ready for guests so far, but wow, it's really something in there."

Jill giggled. "Sounds amazing. I'd love to see it. Do you enjoy working for Mrs. Keslar?"

"Oh, sure. She's a little quirky." Olive waved her hand to brush aside that concern. "But don't pay any attention to that stuff. She's really a lot of fun."

Jill nodded.

"Well, I've got to be getting back, but I would really like to use your restroom before I leave if it's okay. I'm sorry to ask, but the cold just does something to me!" Olive fanned herself with her hand. "I don't know why."

"No problem at all. They are right over there on the side of the waiting room." Jill pointed.

"I'll just be a minute!" Olive scurried off as Jill rolled her eyes and smiled. The girl was a bundle of energy. She might just make an excellent spin instructor.

§

Conrad shut down his computer and reached for his jacket. It was time to head home to get cleaned up for the party. He'd come into the office just to finish up a couple of things that were left behind Friday afternoon, but one thing led to another. Now it was late afternoon, and he had to pick up Cora Mae in a couple of hours. Pulling his office door shut, he heard whistles and shouts coming from the lobby. Officer Crawford was whistling with his fingers in his mouth and Conrad could see Harold "Wink" Hobson who had just come on duty for the night shift. He was also whistling and clapping.

"What's all the ruckus?" Conrad shouted as he walked down the hallway.

Wink pointed across the lobby to Detective Sam Snell. Sam had just walked in the front doors in a black suit and tie with a white shirt, which had made him a target for teasing from the other officers.

"Aren't you spiffy?!" Officer Tabor chuckled as he slipped his coat on.

"You're going to the party tonight too, aren't you, Officer London?" Sam smiled.

"I am! In fact, I'm just getting off, so I was going home to get ready, but I don't have anything as pretty as all that to wear," Tabor teased.

"It's not the suit that matters. It's how you wear the suit!" Sam adjusted his tie and yanked on each cuff.

"You look nice, Sam. I was just headed home to get changed myself." Conrad raised an eyebrow at Wink to dismiss the childishness.

"I don't want to hold you up, but I got the film back finally and wanted to show you what they found."

"It's about time!"

"I'll walk you out." Sam pulled the lobby door open and held it for Conrad. "There were only four shots taken on the roll. She didn't have any other film on her, which I thought was odd. Most people going out on a long walk to shoot pictures would have taken an extra roll in their pocket, don't you think? We never found any."

"That would seem normal." Conrad zipped his coat as Sam handed him the four photographs.

Conrad squinted. "That's Peter! Is this the storage building by the back fence?"

"Yes, it's the back property line for the mine. That building is a special chemical storage unit where they have to lock up the ammonium nitrate explosives." Sam tapped his finger on the photograph of a small metal building. "It's not combustible on its own, but you have to keep it separate from combustible materials to be safe."

"That's the stuff everybody thinks is dynamite." Conrad nodded. "So, what is Peter doing here? It looks like he's removing it and putting it in a truck."

"Yeah, keep going." Sam pointed at the photos. "See the next one? That's Noah."

"Well, I'll be! And who is the little guy by the truck door?" Conrad turned the photo around to show Sam.

"That is David Dorn. He was an apprentice to Noah Yates. He left town three days ago though. He finally got his blaster certification and got a job in Virginia."

"So, what do you make of all this?" Conrad handed the photos back to Sam and reached for his car door.

"I think Peter and Noah are stealing explosives." Sam crossed his arms over his chest. "I've got a couple of deputies looking for Noah now and I'd like to talk to Peter, too. His mother claims she hasn't seen him since the funeral, but I don't believe her."

"If Peter had disappeared yesterday and not come home, Mother Jessup would have been down here filing a report!" Conrad huffed. "There's no way she'd let that go."

"Exactly. She was cool as a cucumber when she said he was missing. She knows where he is. She's just not telling me."

"Did the mine report a theft?" Conrad frowned. "Have you talked to Walter to see if he can confirm whether there is anything missing?"

"He's not going to want to rat on his own kid!" Sam said. "Regardless, we can't find him either. I left a message at the mine's corporate office about a possible theft and they're trying to find Walter."

“Sam, this is a serious public safety issue. We can’t have this kind of explosive just out in the community in the hands of an untrained person!” Conrad tossed both hands up in the air. “You’ve got to notify ATF!”

“I have, Chief. I called the Bureau of Alcohol, Tobacco, Firearms and Explosives. My office sent them copies of our files and they are sending an officer out of Columbus, so it will probably be tomorrow before they get here. I’d like to have someone for them to interview when they do show up.”

“Let me go back inside and update Wink. He can keep an eye out for them tonight and brief the night shift on it. Walter should be performing in the community play tonight. There’s a seven o’clock show, so I’ll get one of my guys to check down there. He might even show up at the Keslar party after the play and if so, we’ll see him.”

“Good idea. Thanks, Chief. See you at the party!”

Sheri Richey

Chapter 26

Rosa Newberg, finally comfortable in her new identity as Olive, stood in the grand foyer of the Keslar mansion waiting for the first guests to arrive. Grace Keslar was back in the kitchens looking over everyone's shoulder and inspecting the offerings, so she had directed Olive out front. She wanted each guest to receive a personal greeting when they arrived. Thumper was handling the coat check and Alice was in charge of the servers.

Christmas music sung by The Legends blasted from speakers on the side of the building and the front steps glowed with rows of twinkling tiny white lights. Bing Crosby, Perry Como and Andy Williams were playing on a looped recording that Mrs. Keslar had piped throughout the house all week. Although Olive had never heard of some of the artists, she now could sing along to every song.

Despite the unease of having her name changed to Olive and the disappointment of being assigned floors to clean, she had enjoyed her unorthodox situation at the Keslar mansion. She thought Mrs. K was happy with her and she had learned many things about the Keslar family and the beautiful home.

"Hi, Jill!" Olive held the door open for Jill Seabrook to step inside. "You are our first guest tonight. It's good to see you again."

"Good evening, Olive. It's good to see you, too. I came early in hopes I could chat with Mrs. Keslar for just a few minutes before people start showing up. Do you think she can spare me a minute?"

"Let me go check for you. It may be hard to pull her out of the kitchen, but I'll let her know you are here."

"Thank you."

Olive left Jill in the foyer and shuffled back toward the kitchen with care. Mrs. Keslar had given her a long dress to wear, but the high heeled shoes had proved to be too much of a challenge. To keep her from falling, Mrs. Keslar had gotten her some flats to wear, which made the dress a little too long. They decided it was safer to trip on the dress than to fall off of the shoes, but either way, she had to concentrate when she walked.

"Miss Trawl, Jill is here and would like to speak with you. She's out in the foyer."

"Oh! Yes, I need to talk to her, too. Here!" Grace thrust a long wooden spoon in front of Olive's face. "Take care of this for me, please."

Grace pushed through the kitchen door and Olive looked at Dorothy Parrish. After a moment of Olive holding the spoon upright like a torch, they both laughed. "I guess I need to find a place for this." Olive placed it on the edge of the sink.

Dorothy shook her head. "What did you call her?

Miss Trawl?"

"Oh, it's some French word. I don't know what it means." Olive shrugged. "Do you need any help? Do you have everything?"

"Yeah, I'm fine in here. My husband, Frank, is bringing in the last of it and Imogene is giving the servers their instructions. We are ready to go."

"Great! See you later." Olive pushed the kitchen door open and took her baby steps to the front door. She stood by the window watching for the next guest to arrive.

Jill and Grace were in the study off the foyer and Olive could hear a little of what Mrs. Keslar was saying, but Jill's back was to the door. "That's dreadful! Have you reported this to the police?" Grace sounded distraught and Jill's words were muffled. "Spicetown Police will be here tonight. You can talk to them then."

Mrs. Keslar pulled Jill further into the office and Olive could not hear the rest of the discussion, but guests started to arrive, so she turned her attentions to the front door.

Olive was certain that at least a hundred people had passed by already before she started to feel as though it was slowing down some. Poor Thumper had been drowning in coats in a small room off of the lobby.

"Don't you look pretty tonight!" Sheriff Bobby Bell handed his long black wool coat to Olive as he stepped inside the door. "It smells a little like snow out there. I hope I'm wrong about that, but the wind is kicking up." Bobby fluffed and patted his thick black hair.

"Thank you, Sheriff. Welcome! It's nice and warm in here. Mrs. Keslar has a fire burning in the parlor and there is a lovely array of hors d'oeuvres in the back of the ball room."

"Mighty fine!" Bobby smoothed his lapel with his hand and ambled toward the ballroom with a wave to those calling out a greeting.

Olive gasped when Stanley tapped her on the shoulder from behind. "Mrs. K told me to relieve you. You've been on your feet long enough. Go get yourself something to eat. Alice is coming up to relieve Thumper, too." Stanley pointed down the hall toward the kitchen.

Alice waved.

"Here she comes now. You two go rest and have some fun. The little bacon wrapped garlic Parmesan shrimp are to die for!" Stanley whispered and then laughed at his own dramatic delivery.

"Ooh! Sounds wonderful! I can't wait." Olive curled a finger at Thumper to follow. "Let's go, girl."

"Did he say when we need to come back?" Thumper shuffled behind her, and they weaved between the crowded entry area. The ballroom was filling with a hum from dozens of mini conversations sprinkled in every corner. Olive walked around the edges of the room to inch closer to the long banquet tables along the walls.

"Stanley didn't say we had to come back." Olive shrugged. "This room is just amazing. It looks so different decorated and full of people."

"I love all the Christmas music. I thought it was going to drive me crazy at first, but it actually just makes things fun. I love that she plays it during the day."

After filling her plate and looking around, Olive pointed. "There are some chairs free on the side. Do you want to go sit over there?" Olive carried her plate and drink over to the side of the ballroom. After creating a table from her lap, she took a sip of her drink. "I invited my boyfriend, but I don't know if he's going to make it. He said he had to work late. I think he just didn't want to put on a suit."

Thumper giggled. "My mom was invited. I'm sure she's here somewhere by now, but I haven't seen her. Most of these people I don't know."

"Me either. I know the Sheriff." Olive pointed at Bobby Bell. "And that guy over there," Olive pointed at Ted Parish. "He owns Chervil Drugstore. My aunt works there."

Thumper nodded. "That lady, is she waving at you?"

"Yeah!" Olive waved back. "That's the lady that runs Mrs. K's spa. Her name is Jill. She's really nice."

"I think she wants to talk to you."

§

"That's where we stand now." Conrad said after he shared the recent news from Sam Snell with Cora.

"So, you've had a really eventful twenty-four hours!" Cora Mae shook her head as Conrad nodded. "I did hear about the funeral because Amanda came back to work afterwards. She originally planned to go over to Mother Jessup's house, but after Peter ran off, it was canceled so she just came back to work."

"That was unfortunate. It was over by the time I showed up."

"There are still a lot of loose ends to tie up," Cora said as she smiled and waved to someone across the room.

"Sam has referred all the issues to his lieutenant, and it's in their hands now. I can only hope they take the situation seriously. Those items have to be found immediately." Conrad raised his eyebrows to sidestep directly saying the word, explosives. Although they were speaking in low voices, there were people on every side of them.

"What about the mine? Any response from their corporate office regarding the flyrock?"

"No, and I hope you haven't mentioned that to anyone. I didn't realize when I shared that with you that Sam had not told the victim's family. He's submitted his reports to the lieutenant, but he's not been given clearance to tell anyone."

"I haven't said a word, but I'd like to know how they get anything accomplished at the Sheriff's Office. Do they play mother-may-I with every employee?" Cora huffed. "That's ridiculous. Sam should have been free to update the family and file a report with the State. That's his job."

"I agree. Both of those things have to be done. They aren't optional."

"I wonder if it is just this case." Cora smirked.

"It could be Sam." Conrad shrugged. "Or Sam's relationship with Gwen. Those things may color Bobby's directives."

"Eh, it could be you." Cora poked her finger into Conrad's chest. "I keep telling you, he has unresolved issues with you. I don't know if he's afraid of your judgment or he's trying to impress you, but he's uncomfortable around you."

"We have history." Conrad chuckled.

"He's standing right over there, and he hasn't even said hello to us."

"I consider that an early Christmas gift!"

Cora chuckled.

"Where's your little buddy, Walter?" Conrad glanced around the room. "Sam hasn't been able to reach him."

Cora ignored the question. "Have you seen Saucy? The play should be over by now. Oh! There he is." Cora Mae pointed and then waved when Saucy made eye contact with her. He's got his Christmas attire on." Cora chuckled when she saw Saucy's bow tie twinkle from battery operated lights. As usual, he was the talk of the party.

Sheri Richey

Chapter 27

"Olive, can I talk to you for a minute?" Jill Seabrook apologized for interrupting. "Can we step into the hall where it's not so loud?" The Christmas music had been turned up and several couples were dancing.

"Are you having a good time? Isn't the house just so beautiful?" Olive's eyes were wider than her smile. "I just love being here. Everyone is so jealous when I tell them where I work." Olive sighed.

"Yes, it is a magnificent house. Truly one of a kind!" Jill crossed her arms over her chest. "It sounds like you're very happy in your job."

"Mrs. Keslar is very nice." Olive nodded. "You'll like working with her. She seems a little unusual at first, but she's really pretty fantastic."

"Well, I was talking with Mrs. Keslar earlier, because a situation has come up out at the spa. It was a surprise to us, but it turns out that I no longer have an assistant."

"Oh, no! I can't believe anyone would quit before

the spa even opens."

"Actually, it's even worse. It turns out the young woman stole some money from us and has run off. I think her boyfriend has gotten into some trouble and she's trying to help him, but even if she's found, we can't take her back. She's not the type of person we want in a responsible position like assistant manager."

"No, absolutely not. That's terrible so close to opening. You need help getting things ready. I could help you. I don't mind. Mrs. Keslar usually lets me go around four o'clock and I could come out there to help you set up things."

"That's what I wanted to talk to you about. I talked to Mrs. Keslar and although she loves having you at her house, she thinks you could be a very good candidate to take the job of assistant manager at the wellness center. I will show you—"

"What!" Olive grabbed Jill's arms and squeezed as she squealed at such a high pitch the cat was surely to object. "I can't believe this. Really? Do you really mean it? I could work out there as an assistant manager. Really?"

Jill laughed as Olive bounced up and down pushing off Jill's arm as she tried to take her hands.

Suddenly Olive's mouth dropped open, and she gasped. After a long pause, she said, "Oh, no! Oh, no. No! I've messed up. Really bad. I don't know what to do. I can't believe this."

Jill grabbed Olive's arms. "What? What's wrong?"

"Oh, it's bad. It's really bad." Olive looked in the ballroom and turned around to look down the hallway toward the front door. "My boyfriend, I don't think he's here, but he gave me this thing to take... Oh, look!" Olive pointed into the ballroom. "Officer

London is in there. Maybe he can help. What time is it? There's not much time. Let me get him." Olive cupped her hand to tell Jill to follow, and she dove into the crowded ballroom excusing herself with every bump and disheveled maneuver until she reached the side of Officer London, also known as Eugene Tabor.

"Excuse me," Olive said with a bashful curtsy to Eugene who was talking with Sam Snell and Gwen Kimball. "I need your help. My boyfriend had me take this thing out to the wellness spa and it's going to go off at midnight."

Sam Snell stepped forward and put his hand on Olive's upper arm. "Did you say go off?"

"Yeah," Olive said looking at Tabor. "It's just supposed to mess up the bathroom. That's where I put it. It can't hurt anyone. It's just to keep it from opening on time."

Sam grabbed her hand and dragged her through the crowd.

Gwen and Jill hurriedly followed while Officer Tabor went over and tapped Conrad's arm. "Chief! You gotta come!"

Conrad frowned, but saw the progression headed toward the hallway and quickly followed Eugene Tabor through the crowd.

Cora Mae glanced around and rather than stand there alone, decided to follow the train of people leading out of the ballroom.

Gathering in a circle in the hallway, Sam put his hand on Olive's shoulder and hunched his shoulders to look Olive directly in the eye. "I'm Detective Snell and I work for the county sheriff's department. I need you to be clear. Are you saying that there is an explosive device out at the Wellness Center?"

"Yeah! It's just a little thing, and it's in the bathroom. We gotta get it out."

Sam looked at Conrad. "I'm going to call it in. We need the bomb squad. Can you see about getting keys to get us inside?"

Jill popped her head up over Olive's shoulder. "I've got keys. I'll go with you."

"Let me call Wink. My officers are closer." Conrad pulled his phone out of his pocket. "What time? Do you know when it's supposed to go off?"

"Midnight!" Olive held up her index finger. "That's what he said because nobody would be there. It's not meant to hurt anybody."

Conrad put his phone to his ear waiting for Officer Hobson to pick up. "You stay here with her," Conrad pointed at Tabor and Olive.

"Okay, Chief. I can get a statement." Tabor nodded at Olive.

"I'm taking you with me." Conrad pointed at Jill.

"I'll get my coat!" Jill took off down the hallway toward the foyer.

Conrad looked at Cora. "I'll be back."

Cora nodded discreetly and patted Olive's hand. "Maybe we could go sit in the parlor?"

"We'll be right behind you," Sam said glancing at Gwen.

§

"Come on in here, dear. We can sit by the fire." Cora Mae glanced at Eugene Tabor as he followed. "I know Officer Tabor will need to gather some information, but we might as well be comfortable while we do that."

"Officer Tabor?" Olive frowned. "I thought your name was London."

"That's just my Mrs. Keslar name." Eugene chuckled.

Cora Mae pulled a notebook and pen from her large purse and handed it to Eugene.

"Oh, well, my Mrs. Keslar name is Olive, but I'm really Rosa Newberg. Or at least I used to be. Lately, I've started thinking my name is really Olive." Olive tapped the palm of her hand on her forehead.

"Is your mother's name Kay?" Cora's brow lifted. "Did she used to work at the bank?"

"Yeah, she did!"

"Oh, I know your mother then! How nice. Please tell her I said hello when you see her."

"I will. She's retired now, but she's busier than ever."

"I hear a lot of people say that happens." Cora smiled at Olive but saw Tabor scowl.

"So, Rosa, who is your boyfriend now?"

"Noah Yates. We've only been dating a few weeks. He's new to town." Olive glanced through the parlor door to the foyer. "I invited him tonight, but he said he had something to do. I don't think he had anything to wear. I didn't either. Mrs. Keslar got me this dress." Olive pinched the fabric on her legs.

"It's very pretty."

"Thank you. I liked it, too. Mrs. Keslar is so generous."

Cora Mae smiled. "Now, did your boyfriend, Noah, tell you why he wanted to damage the restroom in the spa?"

"He said it was a job. I don't really know anything about his work."

"You mentioned he wanted to delay the opening of the spa," Tabor scooted to the edge of his chair. "Was that his job? Was his job to delay the opening?"

"Yeah, I think so. He told me not to worry. It was safe. It was just a little thing." Olive held her hands about fifteen inches apart. "He said it would be loud, but that no one would get hurt."

"You left this explosive in the bathroom out there today?" Cora said.

"This morning when I took a package to Jill." Olive folded her hands in her lap. "Jill gave me a tour of the spa while I was there. It's a wonderful place."

"What made you decide to tell us about it tonight?" Tabor said.

"Jill offered me a job out there. I'm so excited about it. I love the spa and I was planning to join when it opened. That's when I realized that if the restrooms were ruined, I wouldn't have a job. I don't really think it's right to ruin the restrooms anyway. Noah's done some other things out there to stop the opening. I don't know who he works for, but they don't want the spa to open."

"We're glad you told someone about it, too, but we don't want anyone to get hurt. You're sure that it's not going off until midnight?" Tabor looked at Cora with concern.

"That's what he said. Noah said no one would ever be around at midnight so it was safe."

"Did Noah make this bomb? Is that what he does for work?" Cora tilted her head quizzically.

"I don't know," Olive frowned. "He didn't say. I guess so, though. It's not like you can just go buy one." Olive rolled her eyes. "He's very smart. I'm sure he knows how."

“How did you meet Noah? Were you already working for Mrs. Keslar when you met?” Cora reached in her purse for her phone when she heard the vibration.

“No, but he’s the one that recommended I apply out here. He said it was a great job, and he was right. It’s been so much fun.”

“If you like Mrs. Keslar,” Tabor said with a scowl. “Why would you let Noah do something to hurt her business? You know she owns the spa, right? He was trying to damage her business.”

“Noah said she had insurance that would pay for it and there would be no harm done. He was just doing his job. It wasn’t personal.” Olive shrugged.

“Well, hopefully they can prevent it from damaging anything.” Cora reached over and patted Olive’s hand. “Would you like something to drink, dear? Maybe some punch?”

Olive nodded.

“I think I’m going to get myself some. I’ll be right back.”

Cora had received a text from Conrad saying he had arrived at the spa and asking Cora to tell Tabor to detain Walter or Noah for questioning if either of them were at the party.

Cora stepped around the corner and into the hallway with her phone in her hand and sent a reply to Conrad.

I know Walter has been at the party tonight. I’ll look for him.

Sheri Richey

Chapter 28

“You can’t just go charging in there!” Sam Snell shouted with his hands in the air. “The bomb squad has been called. We have to wait for them.”

Conrad scowled. Wink had his hand on the front door ready to pull it open as soon as Jill had it unlocked. Wink looked back at Conrad waiting for direction and released the door handle. “Okay, but it seems silly for us all to rush out here and just stand by.”

Conrad nodded in agreement. If the spa had been in his jurisdiction, they would have already brought the bomb out, but he couldn’t take control of the scene. “This isn’t a Spicetown call, Wink. If the county wants to wait, we have to wait.”

Wink nodded and walked toward his cruiser. “If you don’t need me then, Chief, I’ll go back on patrol.”

“You aren’t going in?” Jill Seabrook reached for the door handle. “I’ll go inside then. I can at least look and see where it is."

"No! If fact, we all need to get further from the building. We don't know how much blast it has."

"Wink, why don't you take Ms. Seabrook back to the Keslar Mansion. I'll get your keys back to you after this situation is resolved." Conrad pointed at Wink. "Officer Hobson can give you a ride. Detective Snell is right. It's not safe to be out here right now."

Jill frowned and glanced back at the building indecisively.

Conrad reached out for her arm. "You can fill Mrs. Keslar in on what's happening. I'm sure it would be difficult to get her on the phone right now with the party going on and she should be kept informed."

Jill nodded her acceptance and reluctantly walked toward Wink's car.

"What time did she visit this morning?" Conrad called out as Jill opened the car door. "Do you recall about what time she arrived?"

"It was about 10:30 I think."

"Thank you." Conrad waved as Jill got into Wink's car. "I'm just wondering if the timer was set for twelve hours, and the young lady thought it meant midnight when she saw it." Conrad shrugged. "If so, we only have a half an hour."

Sam moaned and reached for his phone. "Let me get an ETA from them."

When Sam stepped away to place his call, Gwen Kimball looked at Conrad. "Chief, maybe I should just run in there."

"No," Conrad said with a shake of his head. "If anybody goes, it'll be me. I'll give Sam a little while to do the official thing, but I'm not going to sit here and let the place blow up because of protocol."

"But it's only ten o'clock now— "

"But it could blow at any time. I don't think the young lady knows what she planted. It could even be set to detonate when it's moved or dropped. We don't know enough, and guessing is a bad idea."

"I could take a look and see if there's a timer visible. I wouldn't touch anything."

"No. Sam is going to get into enough trouble for not telling the Sheriff before we left the party." Conrad smirked. "We don't want to cause him any more. Even if we brought the bomb outside, we don't have any appropriate place to put it where it can blow safely. It's best to wait on the county's bomb experts. They just need to hurry."

"I hope Mrs. Keslar has the place insured," Gwen muttered.

§

"Walter! I've been looking for you." Cora bumped elbows with Walter Slope when she stepped up beside him at the drink bar. "I thought certain you had planned to attend this wonderful event, but I knew you had the play earlier tonight."

"Good evening, Cora Mae. It's wonderful to see you. I'm so glad you found me. It's so crowded in here; I don't know that I would have ever located you."

"How did the play go this evening? Did everything run smoothly?"

'Oh, yes. It's a delightful story. Have you seen it yet?"

"No, I haven't. My tickets are for tomorrow's matinée performance." Cora picked up a small plate and chose a white chocolate covered treat for her snack. "Have you been here long?"

"Ah, no. No, I haven't. Just got here."

"Mmm, these are quite good." Cora held up her candied treat and pointed at the display.

"I never eat before a performance, so I'm quite hungry now. Thank you."

"Mayor?" Cora had waved to Officer Tabor when she caught his eye.

"Officer Tabor, hello. Have you met Walter Slope?" Cora presented Walter with a game show wave of her hand and smiled. Tabor had been unable to help her look for Walter since they hadn't met.

"I haven't," Eugene extended his hand for Walter to shake. "Eugene Tabor. It's nice to meet you."

"My pleasure," Walter said with a shrug because he held a plate and a serving spoon in his hands, so he was unable to respond to Eugene's offered hand.

"Where is your young lady?" Cora asked Eugene.

"Oh, I called Officer Reynolds, and he came to give her a ride."

Cora Mae nodded. "Do you know Rosa Newberg, Walter?"

"No, I don't believe so." Walter popped a small cube of cheese into his mouth.

"Hmm, she was here earlier. She works for Mrs. Keslar." Cora put her plate on the table and reached for a napkin. "She was looking for Noah Yates. Have you seen him at the party?"

"No." Walter frowned and shook his head. "But I just got here. I haven't had time to walk around yet."

Cora nodded. "Well, Ms. Newberg said that your son, Noah, was her boyfriend, so I thought perhaps you had met her before."

Although Walter tried to hide the discomfort he felt at Cora's disclosure, he wasn't successful. "No."

"I was rather surprised you hadn't mentioned something to me earlier about your son being in the area. That must be very nice for you." Cora was certain Walter had specifically said he had no children at all when they first met.

"Do you have any idea where your son, Noah, is right now, Mr. Slope?"

"No, I haven't seen him today." Walter turned away from the banquet table and inched away from Cora Mae.

"I need for you to come down to the station. The Chief has asked me to bring you down tonight if I could locate you. You're welcome to take your plate with you if you want, but my car is right outside. I'll drive you."

"What? No. Not right now. I'll come by later and see the Chief. Perhaps Monday would be more convenient."

"No, I'm sorry, but it can't wait." Tabor took Walter's elbow discreetly and Cora tried not to look as smug as she felt.

"Are you arresting me, young man? Because if you aren't, I suggest you take your hand off me."

"No sir. I'm trying to get your help in dealing with a matter at the mine and a criminal report involving your son. It isn't appropriate to discuss it here, and the Chief said you would want to be involved. He talked with the county's detective and there have been some developments that they haven't updated you on."

"Well, what is it? Tell me!"

"He just asked me to bring you to the station. You

will have to talk with him. I'm sorry, but I wasn't there when he—"

"Oh, for heaven's sake!" Walter slammed his plate down on the table and ignoring Cora Mae, he stomped off to the coat check.

Tabor smiled at Cora Mae when she chuckled. "Can you text the Chief and tell him I'm headed in with him?"

"I'm happy to." Cora winked as Tabor turned to follow Walter through the crowd.

§

"Thank you, Captain." Sam Snell waved as the bomb squad slammed the van door to the mobile unit and prepared to leave. They had removed the device and detonated it in a safe container. Now they were taking it back to have it examined by a lab.

Gwen had taken Conrad's squad car back to the party and taken Cora Mae home before getting herself to bed.

"They did a great job," Conrad said as he removed his foot from the bumper of Sam's car where he'd been leaning. "It's been a late night though." It had taken several hours to secure the site, and the night wasn't over yet.

"It has, Chief. Time to go home and get some rest." Sam yawned.

"No can do – We've got Walter Slope to talk to." Conrad stretched his arms over his head.

"I've not gotten clearance to talk to him about the mine theft yet." Sam checked his phone. "I don't think my Lieutenant has even filed the report with the State."

“Maybe not, but I don’t work for your Lieutenant and I’m gonna forget you said that to me.” Conrad smiled. “Don’t worry. I’ll only use it if I need it, but we need to find Noah as soon as possible and I think Walter can help us there.”

“You think he’d roll on his own son!” Detective Snell pushed out his bottom lip and shook his head. “I think we’re wasting our time there.”

“We don’t know until we ask. I have a feeling that old Walter cares more about saving his own tookus than he does about a son that he keeps a secret from everyone, so” Conrad shrugged his shoulders. “I’m going to give it a go!”

Sheri Richey

Chapter 29

"The rental company should be here any minute," Stanley said leaning against the window frame in the Keslar mansion kitchen. "Then we can get these tables out of here and get back to normal."

"My kitchen is a mess," Imogene said as she dunked a tea bag into Mrs. Keslar's cup.

"Last night was fun," Stanley said with a lack of enthusiasm.

"But I'm glad it's over!"

Stanley chuckled. "I could sure use a cup of coffee."

"You'll have to get it yourself. I've got to take Mrs. K her tea. She's in the parlor and she's really troubled right now."

"About Olive?" Stanley shook his head. "I'm pretty disappointed in her, too."

"She did confess though," Imogene soothed. "And she did it before any harm was done."

"I don't think the police that spent all night out at the spa would agree with you." Stanley snorted.

"Waste of resources and it's no fun to spend your night thinking you might blow up."

"I know. You're right." Imogene reneged. "I'm just glad everyone was safe in the end."

"For the moment." Stanley crossed his arms over his chest. "I hope they find the guy soon. Until they do, we need to keep an eye on things. It sounds like this guy is targeting Mrs. K."

"Well, I can't do the sheriff's job. I've got my own work to do. I trust you will go all G.I. Joe on them if any bad guys show up." Imogene winked at Stanley as she backed through the swinging kitchen door with Mrs. Keslar's tea tray in her hands. Although her remarks were made in jest, Imogene knew that Grace Keslar's husband, Chancellor, had hired Stanley for a reason, and it was something more than gardening.

"Here you go," Imogene said softly as she placed the tray on the small table in front of Grace Keslar. Chauncey, the large gray crazy whiskered cat squeaked a small sound out in response. The cat was extremely talkative but did not speak the usual meow language.

"Thank you, Imogene." Grace motioned for her to sit down. "I just got off the phone with Police Chief Harris. He said he isn't in charge of any of this because the spa is outside of Spicetown, but they did do some questioning at his station last night, so he knows they've talked to the bomber's girlfriend and his dad. They still haven't found him though."

"The girlfriend is Olive?"

"Yes, poor child. I don't know how she got herself so tangled up in such a mess."

Imogene huffed.

"They talked to her last night and released her, but

the Chief said that he thinks the county will file charges against her. She's coming by this morning to bring back the evening dress and shoes I loaned to her last night."

"I need to let Stanley know. Do you want to see her when she comes by?"

"No. She said she just wanted to drop them off and that she'd come to the back kitchen door. I don't think she wants to see me. There's nothing really to say at this point. I can't keep her on at the house or give her the spa job. It's so unfortunate, but we'll have to wait and see what happens."

"So, she doesn't know where her boyfriend is? She hasn't heard from him? It seems odd that he isn't wondering why the place didn't blow up last night."

"Speaking of that, the Chief also said the bomb squad's report mentioned that the bomb was strong enough to have ruined the entire facility if it had detonated. Olive thought it was just a little thing, but she was misinformed. I hope she stays away from this boy if he does try to reach out to her. He put her life in real danger!"

"Did the Chief say whether they know why the young man wanted to ruin your spa?"

Grace shook her head. "I don't think they know why."

"Maybe it's not personal, then." Imogene shrugged. "Maybe he's interested in the location or doesn't want a spa to come to town. You know I told you from the beginning that your business could hurt some other businesses around here. Maybe he's linked to—"

"Sorry to interrupt," Stanley said as he walked in the room. "Miss Olive is in the kitchen. Do you need her for anything?"

"No, dear." Grace said. "She's just returning the clothing she borrowed."

"Oh, okay. Just checking. Oh! It looks like the rental van is pulling in the drive now." Stanley pointed at the windows behind Mrs. Keslar. "They're picking up the tables. I'll go let them in the back."

"Thank you."

"I'll go see Olive," Imogene said as she stood up. "I'll be back with some breakfast for you."

Chauncey said, "Yow."

"Not you, silly." Imogene muttered as she walked back to the kitchen.

Stanley had pushed the kitchen door to stay open and two young men in gray coveralls were in the hall entrance door to the dining room breaking down the folding legs to the long banquet tables.

"Where's Olive?"

"Oh, she left." Stanley pointed to a bag on the counter. "The shoes and dress are inside."

"Did you check the bag for contraband?" Imogene giggled and looked out the window. "I'm disappointed I missed her. How did she look? Is she okay?"

"I did check the bag, and she looked fine considering she tried to blow up a business yesterday." Stanley growled. "I hope she doesn't come back."

"She's just a confused kid." Imogene shook her head as the men walked by with two long tables.

"Is Mrs. Keslar doing okay?"

"She seems to be. She's disappointed in Olive, but she feels like she can't employ her until all of this is settled."

The two men traveled back through the kitchen to the dining room again.

"What do you mean, until it's settled?" Stanley shouted. "She can't seriously be considering ever—"

"This is the last of it." The men walked through the kitchen door, each carrying one end of the long table and headed for the back door. "Have a good day."

"Thank you. You, too." Imogene waved and removed the hold on the swinging kitchen door. "I need to get Mrs. K some breakfast."

Stanley removed the hold on the back door that was keeping it open and went back to the window once he had secured the lock. Peering out of the window he saw Olive standing in the driveway looking at the back of the rental company van. "Olive is still standing out there."

"Tell her to come in!" Imogene said over her shoulder. "I'll get her a cup of coffee."

"Wait, no. She's talking to one of the delivery guys. I guess she knows one of the young men." Stanley continued to watch from the window, ignoring Imogene's request to invite Olive inside, and he saw one of the young men cupping Olive's cheeks in his hands and kissing her. "Hey! That must be Olive's boyfriend!"

Imogene dropped her spatula. "Where?"

"Wait!" Stanley tried to get the back door unlocked quickly, but in his flurry, he locked and unlocked the deadbolt twice before realizing the doorknob itself was locked also.

Imogene went to the window. "He just jumped in the van and they're pulling away."

"Call the police! I'm going to try to catch them."

§

"These are good seats!" Conrad leaned one way and then the other to slip his arm out of his coat and then helped Cora get her arms out also. They had about fifteen minutes before the play began and the community center auditorium was alive with chatter. "Maybe the matinée wasn't the best idea though."

"Why do you say that?" Cora Mae rocked back in surprise.

"All of the kids." Conrad frowned. Children were running in the aisles and scooting down the rows. He couldn't imagine they could keep from squirming throughout the performance.

"I just thought we'd see the best performance if we waited until the end of the run. On opening night, they are too nervous."

"I hope it's good. Wake me up if I fall asleep."

Cora Mae jabbed him in the ribs with her elbow and he chuckled. "What time did you get finished last night?"

"I got home about two o'clock in the morning. Walter wasted about half an hour being mad at me. He's definitely got an angry side to him."

"Yes. I discovered that also." Cora Mae huffed.

"Once he finally calmed down, he told me pretty much what I needed to know."

"Which was?" Cora Mae leaned closer. "Did he know where Noah was?"

"He gave me some ideas, some places to look, but it seems they really don't have much of a relationship. I think Noah took advantage of Walter to get the blaster job."

"That's a shame." She was also ashamed that part of her thought maybe he deserved the mistreatment for not claiming his own child.

"Walter said he's tried over the years to get close to Noah, but they've never really gotten there. He did tell us where he was staying and gave us a couple of contacts to check with."

"I wonder why he kept him a secret."

"My guess would be that the mine probably frowns on nepotism. They might not have let Walter hire him if they'd known or maybe he didn't want the other miners to know."

"So, you don't think he was involved in the theft at all?" Cora raised her eyebrows and sighed. "I'm not so sure about that. I learned quickly to question Walter's character. He is very convincing and can seem sincere, but it's all an act."

"You think he might be in on it?"

"You cannot trust his word," Cora said stabbing the air with her index finger. "He stood right there last night and let me believe he had just come from this play performance, yet he didn't show last night either. Eleanor told me he came to every practice, and not a single performance. Then he told me he'd just arrived, when I saw his toothpicks in the parlor, so I know that wasn't true either. Why lie? People that lie for no reason are the most worrisome."

"Indeed," Conrad chuckled.

"Shhhh," Cora Mae hushed him when Eleanor Cline, high school drama teacher and community center play director, walked out on the stage.

"Good afternoon, everyone. We are happy to have you at our final performance of Comfort Falls Christmas. I have one announcement before we begin. Calvin Watson will be playing the part of Sam, the owner of the barbershop, this afternoon. Please sit back and relax. We hope you enjoy our little production and Happy Holidays to you all."

After the applause, Cora tapped her finger on the program showing the owner of the barbershop was supposed to be played by Walter Slope. Conrad scowled.

A hush fell over the crowd as a soft blue light began to glow to the left of the stage and music started to play. Even before the lyrics began, the familiar tune of Silent Night was recognized by all. A soft male tenor began to sing the favorite song as the play director, Eleanor Cline, came to a podium with a folder in her hand to open the play with narrative background.

The blue light brightened, and Cora Mae clutched Conrad's forearm when she saw the source of the soft tenor voice. Harvey "Saucy" Salzman was standing on the side of the stage at a microphone.

Eleanor waited for the first verse of Silent Night to conclude before she began her opening.

"Today, we're going to take you back. Back to a time right before the Great Depression. December of 1938. It was a mild winter..."

"Saucy," Cora whispered. A tear rolled down Cora's cheek, and the curtain lifted to show the town square of Comfort Falls.

Chapter 30

"I missed having Saucy at Christmas dinner today." Cora stretched her feet out over the ottoman in front of her favorite chair and her big orange cat Marmalade jumped up on her legs.

"I think I ate his share." Conrad patted his stomach. They had moved to the living room to relax after eating. "You shouldn't have made so much since Ned, Saucy and Violet were not coming."

"I don't know how to cook Christmas dinner any other way!" Cora chuckled. "I'll have lots of leftovers."

"I'll certainly do my part to help you manage those." Conrad's stomach shook when he laughed and that made him groan.

"I'm glad we got to see Saucy at the play since he's not here today. I had to give him a big hug. I was so thrilled with the job he did."

Conrad smiled. "I think he really enjoyed himself. Singing seemed to come much easier than the acting. He was relaxed and didn't have to worry about memorizing a script."

"He did well in the part he played, but the singing at the beginning and the end was phenomenal. I can't believe I've known him all these years and had no idea he had such a beautiful voice!"

"I got a kick out of Miriam." Conrad rolled his eyes. Miriam Landry was the president of the Chamber of Commerce in Spicetown, and she was friendly to no one.

"I can finally pay her a compliment. They could not have cast the part of the Widow Jeffries any better. Miriam Landry fit that role perfectly!"

"You're just saying that because she's that person in real life." Conrad laughed.

Cora scrunched her nose in deliberation and then said, "You're probably right. I do wish Walter Slope had shown up. Saucy said he had a beautiful baritone voice, and we really missed something by his absence."

"I wish he would have shown up so I could have arrested him." Conrad huffed. "They did find him. Did I tell you that?"

"Yes. Is he in the county jail?" Cora stroked Marmalade's head as she purred.

"No, he's made a statement and been released. Apparently, Detective Snell said Walter gave up his son." Conrad shook his head. "First, Noah Yates tells them that his dad, Walter, set up the whole thing. He laid it on thick. He was just taking orders from dear old Dad and so he stole the explosives and tried to ruin the spa because Walter made him."

Cora Mae frowned. She thought Walter complicit, but that was more involved than she expected.

"Then Walter puts his statement down that he had

nothing to do with any of it. According to him he is an angel." Conrad chuckled. "Sam was a bit perplexed and locked them both up for a couple of days!"

Cora nodded. "That sounds right."

"Probably the truth is somewhere in the middle. You did say you hoped the two of them found something special to do together for the holidays."

Cora Mae smiled. "I did, didn't I?"

"Well, they had the pictures of Noah that Jane Jessup took, so he couldn't dispute that. Noah is charged with the theft of explosives and the vandalism of the spa. That gave them reason to hang onto him. They made a deal with Walter too soon I think, so he was released."

"So, Walter is getting off scot free?"

"He did lose his job and his pension, if that gives you any comfort. The mine is trying to limit their liability from Jane's death and the attorneys for the mine are trying to hold Walter responsible for not managing the blasting in a safe and legal way. They might have more if they ever find Peter Jessup. He's still in the wind."

"They need to tail his mother!" Cora shook her index finger in Conrad's direction. "She knows where he is and she's in communication with him."

"I agree, but I don't think the sheriff's office has the resources to track him all over the country. They are relying on the mine's big legal firm to hunt for him because they're looking for him, too. I think the girlfriend is with him. She's been charged with theft as well. Apparently, she took money from the spa before they split town."

"And poor Jane Jessup is in the middle of all this chaos. She doesn't even know that her pictures were what revealed all the evil going on. I'm sure that's why she took the photos to start with. She knew what was happening and that her husband was out there helping."

"Yes, but I think the mine will be held accountable for her death. I just don't know what changes that might mean for Spicetown. The people working at the mine…" Conrad shrugged. "For their sake, I hope they don't close, but I'm never going to feel the same about the blasting. I don't think anyone in town ever will again."

"I know it will be more difficult to trust them. This incident definitely destroyed the mine's integrity, but the situation with the sheriff is no different. Anytime the person in charge shows that dishonesty is okay, everyone's understanding of what's acceptable instantly changes. Bobby Bell's actions will have long term repercussions." Cora Mae looked down at her hands in her lap. "It's a sad day for elected officials everywhere."

"There is still a chance that he's being wrongly accused. Noah Yates is the only one saying that Bobby Bell paid him to harm the Irenic Wellness Center. I know the county commissioners have suspended him from duty pending an investigation for corruption, but unless they get more proof, it's a weak case."

"It's the only explanation! Bobby Bell's son may run the gym in Paxton, but I heard that Bobby financed the whole thing." Cora tossed her hands in the air. "Noah has no motive to harm Grace Keslar's new business. Bobby is the only one with something to lose."

"True." Conrad nodded. "If Bobby beats the charge, it will still make it hard for him to be re-elected next time. Sam Snell felt from the beginning that Bobby was involved in this. He just couldn't nail it down."

"You could run." Cora tilted her head and looked over at Conrad. "You could run for sheriff next time. That's a fabulous idea!"

"What?"

"Yes! I could help. I can fix you up with all sorts of people that can help. I know a guy in Paxton who can make your signs and another that does the shirts and hats. Postcards and mailing services are better done through the city though. You just upload your designs, and they even mail them for you. I'll get you the name. They give a good group discount and sending to the entire county is probably a better deal—"

"Cora! I'm not running for sheriff."

"Why not? You'd be perfect and I can help you. I know all the county commissioners and I'll introduce you. Amanda can help with the internet stuff. I have to admit I've never mastered that, but there are plenty of people around that—"

"No! You seem to forget I was in the city. I took this job as Spicetown police chief so I could slow down and ease myself into retirement. I'm not looking for challenges at my age."

Cora took a deep breath. "I understand." Cora glanced guiltily in Conrad's direction. "I'm seriously thinking about retirement myself, so I get it. This has been a very challenging year."

"I think you have another term in you. I would really hate to see you not run one more time."

"I don't know." Cora frowned.

"There's nobody to take your place. I know you've

always hoped Jimmy Kole would step into your role, but I just don't think he's capable. He can't seem to think like a public servant. He's not a leader."

"I've given the issue a lot of study this year, Connie. I won't lie; it makes me very nostalgic, but that's not a good enough reason to run again. Nostalgia is just the mind's way of balancing the complications of the present. The fact that my thoughts and hopes keep going backward, makes me think I'm not ready to face the future. Things are getting too complex. Maybe Spicetown needs someone smarter than me."

"Poppycock!" Conrad said slapping his hand on the arm of the chair.

Cora Mae giggled. "Would you like some more hot chocolate, Connie?" Cora put Marmalade on the ottoman and pushed herself out of her comfy chair. It was time to change the subject.

"I'll just take some chicory coffee and maybe a gingersnap or two."

"There's still pie," Cora called from the kitchen.

"No, I haven't made room for that yet." Conrad chuckled.

"I can put a Christmas movie on, if you like, or we could play a hand or two of gin rummy." Cora carried the coffee and a plate of cookies into the living room.

"Aw, it's Christmas. We can go crazy. Let's just do both!"

∞

★ The Spicetown Star ★

Suspended Sheriff Pleads Guilty

Paxton, Ohio – Suspended County Sheriff Robert Bell pleaded guilty Thursday morning to five counts of his original indictment related to allegations of abuse of his position, tampering with evidence, and theft in office.

After eight months of investigation, the 12 counts of the indictment were dropped in exchange for his guilty plea. Previously suspended Robert Bell has now been terminated from his position as sheriff and disqualified from holding future public office in Ohio.

Bell's felony counts of theft in office and tampering with evidence are related to his admitted use of confiscated drug money to fund a new business venture with his son in Paxton.

Bell will be sentenced at a later date and faces the possibility of eight years in prison.

Sheri Richey

Imogene's Brunswick Stew

- 2 pounds cooked and diced boneless, skinless chicken, pork, or a combination
- 3 (15- to 16-ounce) cans cream-style corn
- 2 to 3 cups diced cooked potatoes
- 1 ½ cups ketchup
- ½ cup barbecue sauce
- 3 to 4 tablespoons bacon drippings
- 2 tablespoons Worcestershire sauce
- ½ teaspoon Kosher salt
- ½ teaspoon freshly ground black pepper
- 1 teaspoon hot sauce, optional
- 1 or 2 tablespoons dried minced onion, optional

Mix all in a stock pot and bring to boil.
Cover and reduce heat to low.
Simmer for 30 minutes.

Sheri Richey

Walter's Cinnamon Toothpicks

- 2 oz. Cinnamon bark oil
- 12-16 oz. Glass, airtight jar with a lid
- 100+ Wooden toothpicks

Fill the jar with at least 2 oz. of the cinnamon bark oil. Make sure that the bottom of the jar is covered with the mixture.

Place as many toothpicks as you can inside the jar. You can add 100 to 500 toothpicks. Just make sure that every single one is standing in the oil.

Once all the toothpicks are inside, seal the jar with the lid. Allow the toothpicks to soak in the mixture for at least 24 hours.

Dry on parchment paper or aluminum foil, not paper towels or napkins. Layout the toothpicks flat and spread them out so they can dry faster.

Once the toothpicks are dry, store them in a sealed container.

Sheri Richey

Did you enjoy meeting Grace Keslar, the eccentric wealthy widow of Keslar Mansion? If you'd like to learn more about Grace (and Chauncey), keep an eye out for **Cat in Cahoots, A Keslar Mansion Mystery**, scheduled for release in 2022!

Sheri Richey

I'd love to hear from you!

Find me on Facebook, Goodreads, Twitter, my website or join my email list for upcoming news!

www.SheriRichey.com